I0535814

The Fiancée

Single Wide Female in Love
Book 3

By

Lillianna Blake

Copyright © 2015 Lillianna Blake

All rights reserved.

ISBN: 0692530258
ISBN-13: 978-0692530252

DEDICATION

To all women out there who are feeling
slightly stressed about an upcoming event.
Don't forget to breathe. ☺

TABLE OF CONTENTS

CHAPTER 1

My reflection was the most satisfying thing I'd ever seen. There before me was the Sammy I'd dreamed of being for so long. In the white wedding gown that I wore, my figure was flattered by the subtle curves of the design of the dress. All of my hard work had paid off. I finally looked the way I'd hoped I would on my wedding day.

"Uh, Sammy, you're going to have to breathe at some point."

The voice of my best friend brought me back to reality. I exhaled and the sucked-in tummy poofed right out. The figure that I saw in the mirror transformed into a roll of fat that threw off the entire look of the dress. In fact, it stretched the intricate lace so much that the pattern was distorted.

"Oh dear." The owner of the boutique tried to pinch some material along my waist.

"Ouch—Gail!" I squirmed away from her touch.

"Sorry." She gulped.

I blinked back tears. Since Max had proposed to me, I might have relaxed about my diet and exercise plan a little too much. I might have celebrated our engagement multiple times with multiple bottles of wine and multiple indulgences. There was no question in my mind that my weight loss had gone awry. It was visible right there in the mirror.

"I must be a little bloated."

"More bloated than the last time we fitted the dress." Gail looked up at me with a frown. "We're going to have to let the dress out a size or two."

"What?" I shook my head. "No, no, no. I wanted to be a certain size on my wedding day, and this dress is that size. We can't let it out."

"Sammy, can you even walk in it?" Stephanie sighed. "I don't want to be harsh, but you have to be able to make it down the aisle, don't you think?"

I scowled in her direction. Yes, I knew she was right. No, I didn't like it. "Do you think it's too late to hire one of those hand-carried sleighs?"

"No, it's probably not too late, but you'll have to stand to exchange your vows."

I sighed. "The last thing I want is to worry about suffocating on my wedding day."

"Not to mention having your circulation cut off." Gail smiled.

"Thanks, thanks for that." I tried not to roll my eyes. "Okay, so new plan. I just have to lose the weight—that's all there is to it. I've done it before. I can do it again."

"What if you can't? Then it will be too late to let out the dress, and you won't have anything to wear." Gail tugged at the waist of the dress again.

"Gee, Gail, you're not jumping on the positive thought bandwagon here, are you?" I batted her hand away from my waist before she could pinch it again.

"I'm just trying to be realistic, Samantha. I've dealt with a lot of brides. It's a very sad thing when their wedding day is ruined because they won't alter their dress. You'll look just as beautiful with it let out. Trust me."

I wanted to believe her, but I had a certain image burned into my mind. It had been there since I was a little girl. I didn't want to change that image.

"Wait, how much time do you need to make alterations?"

"At least two weeks."

"Okay. The wedding is in two months. So I have about six weeks, right?" I forced a smile to my lips. "I can slim down in six weeks. No problem! Right, Stephanie?" I glanced over my shoulder at my friend.

"Oh sure, right." She quirked an eyebrow. "I mean, it takes me a year to lose five pounds, but you're not me. I'm sure you could do it."

I frowned. It wasn't exactly the unwavering support that I'd been hoping for.

"No, I mean it. I really do. I've done it before. Not as fast, of course, but I know I can do it." I looked into the mirror at Gail's reflection. "We'll have another fitting in six weeks. If the dress needs to be let out more, we'll let it out then. If not, then I'll get two weeks to enjoy fitting into my dress."

"If that's what you want." Gail nodded. "You're the bride."

I smiled at her words. I liked how they sounded. I was the bride. I was going to marry the man of my dreams. If that wasn't motivation enough to get my weight loss back on track, I didn't know what would be.

"Sure, I just need to monitor my diet and ramp up my exercise. I'll lose the weight in no time." I stepped away from the mirror. As I did, I caught a glimpse of my wide round white rump in the dress.

"Oh!" I cringed. "And squats, lots of squats."

"You can do it, Samantha." Stephanie smiled at me. "But even if you can't, Max will still think you are the most beautiful bride that ever walked the face of the earth."

"You're probably right." I laughed.

As I changed out of the dress I knew that Stephanie was right. Max had gushed about my beauty when I was at my heaviest point. But this wasn't about Max—not entirely. It was about me being the bride that I'd always imagined myself being.

Gail collected the dress from me with a wistful smile. "Every time I help a new bride prepare for her wedding it reminds me of my own."

"Was it everything that you'd hoped for?" My heart swelled at the thought of it.

"Oh no, not at all. It was a disaster." She shook her head. "The cake was knocked over, there was a surprise rainstorm that collapsed the tent on all my guests, and the groom got his shirt stuck in the fly of his pants. I was in tears most of the day."

"That's horrible." My eyes widened at the thought of that happening to me.

"Yes, I thought it was too. But then my husband rescued the minister from under the tent and whisked me away to an old half-collapsed barn on the property, and the moment the minister told him to kiss me, a rainbow sprung across the sky. So to me, it was magical."

I smiled at the sweetness of her memory. I could understand the lesson—that a wedding was about love, not about all the details. But I wanted the details to be perfect too.

"Thanks, Gail. I'll see you in six weeks."

CHAPTER 2

As I left the boutique with Stephanie, the sky rumbled. My attention was drawn to it. It reminded me of the story that Gail had just told.

"I've got to lose the weight, Stephanie."

"I'm sure you will, but try not to forget that you're getting married. It's supposed to be fun." She gave me a quick hug. "I'd better run before I get caught in this rain. Where are you headed?"

"Dinner with Max."

"Wonderful! Have fun!" She waved to me as she walked around the boutique to the parking lot.

I knew that I should rush to my car too, but my mind was on the sky. The way the dark clouds rolled in seemed like an ominous warning. When a flash of lightning tore across the heavy clouds I jumped and ran for my car.

As I ran, I fumbled for my keys in my purse. I found an old wad of gum, a set of earbuds—that I didn't remember were in there—and some dryer lint from when I worked at Fluff and Stuff. What I did not find were my keys.

Suddenly I remembered that I'd held them in my hand when I went into the fitting room. I must have set them down on the bench in the fitting room instead of putting them in my purse. Stephanie was already gone and I could feel the first drips of the approaching torrential downpour.

I hurried back to the front of the boutique. When I tried to open the door, it wouldn't budge. I saw that the sign had been changed from Open to Closed. I must have been Gail's last appointment.

The sky rumbled again. Rain splashed down on the top of my head. I ran back to my car and checked to see if any of the doors were unlocked. Of course, they were all locked.

The rain began to pour down in sheets. I pulled out my phone and dialed Max's number.

"Hey, babe, I'm waiting for you at the restaurant."

"Well, it might be a while."

"Huh? Why?"

"I'm locked out of my car."

"Oh no! In this rain? I'll come and get you."

"It's okay, you just enjoy your dinner. I'm not far from my apartment. I'm just going to walk home and get my spare key."

"No way, I'm coming to get you."

"Really, Max, it's alright. I can use a walk in the rain."

"Sammy, I'll be there in five minutes."

I sighed and hung up the phone. Max knew me very

well. I would have enjoyed the walk in the rain, but not the lightning in the sky.

I ducked under the awning of the boutique. I watched the other people on the street scramble for cover. Within a few minutes Max's car pulled up right in front of the boutique.

"Need a lift?" He grinned at me through the window.

I scrambled into the car and laughed as I pulled the door shut. "I didn't expect a monsoon. I guess we'll have to stop so I can change."

"You look gorgeous to me." Max leaned over for a kiss. I smiled through it. Max always had a way of making me feel amazing, no matter how self-conscious I'd been the moment before.

"Well, I'd prefer to eat my dinner dry."

"Okay, okay, you can change. But only if I can watch." He winked at me.

"Stop it!" I laughed.

He drove the few minutes to my apartment.

I grabbed dry clothes and rushed into the bathroom to change. As soon as I stepped into the bathroom, my scale greeted me. I stared down at it. I'd been avoiding it lately—most likely because I knew that my diet hadn't been the best and that I'd been skipping my exercise.

But after the morning at the dress fitting, I knew that I needed to have an idea of how much weight I had to lose. I took a deep breath and stepped on the scale. The numbers spun and then settled. I stepped off the scale.

"That can't be right." My heart started to pound. I stepped back onto the scale. The numbers spun and settled again.

"No!" I cringed. I thought maybe I'd gained ten or fifteen pounds, but the scale told me it was closer to twenty. Twenty pounds in six weeks? I groaned and looked away from the number. All of the hard work I'd done and just a few months of slacking off had led to this. I was so disgusted that I couldn't look at myself in the mirror. I pulled my clothes on and sulked my way back to Max.

"Ready to go?" He smiled.

"Sure." I couldn't look at him.

"Great, I'm starving." He grabbed my hand and led me out of the apartment.

CHAPTER 3

When we arrived at the restaurant a gloomy cloud still hung over me. There were so many different emotions rushing through me. I was angry, disappointed, and scared. When I looked at the menu, all the words blurred together. The delicious scents of the food around me were torturous.

I thought about all the people who followed my blog and read my books. What would they think of the mistake that I'd allowed myself to make?

"What are you going to order?" Max peeked over the top of the menu.

"Just some chicken."

"Okay, sounds good. I'm going to have steak." He set the menu down as the waitress approached.

"I'll take the chicken breast, but please hold the sauce."

"I'm sorry, you don't want the sauce?" The waitress looked at me with disbelief.

"That's right, just the chicken, please."

"But, the sauce is what makes the dish." She smiled. "We could always put it on the side."

"No, thank you. No sauce at all, please."

"Sammy, the sauce is fantastic. It's one of your favorite dishes." Max frowned.

"I don't understand why this is a problem. I just want you to hold the sauce, okay?" I raised an eyebrow at the waitress. I didn't need to be reminded of how much I loved that sauce.

"Sure, no problem, you don't have to be rude." The waitress snatched up the menus.

As she walked away Max reached across the table and took my hand.

"You doing okay?"

"Yes."

"Okay." He smiled.

"How are the plans coming for the honeymoon?"

"Honeymoon?" He furrowed an eyebrow. "Is someone getting married?"

"Ha ha." I sighed. "I'm serious, Max. You can't leave that until the last minute. We have to make sure it's ironed out. We only have two months left, you know."

"Sammy, relax." Max patted my hand. "I said I'd handle it, and I will."

I nodded, but I wasn't reassured. Max was very responsible, but I wasn't used to giving up control. He'd asked to plan the honeymoon to take some of the pressure off me, but I wasn't feeling any less pressure. So far, the plans for the wedding had come together easily, but the dress not fitting was a big fat monkey wrench in my plan. I wasn't sure that I was going to be able to lose enough weight to fit into it.

When our food arrived, I was taunted by the scent of butter sauce. I looked down at my plate to see that my chicken was smothered in it.

"Uh, I asked for no sauce."

"I'm sorry, the chef must not have followed my directions." The waitress frowned. "It'll take twenty minutes if we have to make a new plate. Would you like me to send it back?"

"Just eat it, Sammy, you know you'll enjoy it." Max shook his head as he cut into his steak.

I didn't want to be rude. I didn't want to ruin our meal.

"Fine. Okay." I nodded.

"Great." She smiled and walked away.

I pushed the chicken around on my plate. The buttery sauce mocked me.

Max's voice drew me out of my war with my sauce-covered chicken.

"Aren't you hungry?"

"Sure, I just might finish it later."

"Really?" He raised an eyebrow. "Are you sure you're not getting sick?"

"No, I'm not. I just don't want to gorge myself on this overpriced slop." I turned up my nose.

"This is your favorite restaurant." Max frowned. "That's why I invited you here."

"Not tonight it's not."

"Why not? What's wrong?"

"Nothing. I just don't think I like this place any more. Really, it's fine, Max. The company more than makes up for the food."

"Okay." He smiled at me. "How did your dress fitting go? Do I get to see it yet?"

"Don't be silly. You can't see the dress before the day of the wedding. It's bad luck."

"Oh, trust me, if I'm marrying you, it isn't possible for me to have bad luck."

"You mean worse luck?" I stared across the table.

"No! That's not what I meant! I meant, it'll be the luckiest day of my life. No superstition can change that."

"Aw." I grinned at him. "You're so good to me."

"I try." Max finished the last of the food on his plate. He looked over at mine. "Are you really not going to eat that?"

"No." I tried not to make eye contact with the sauce. "No, I'm not."

"Alright, well can I have it? It looks really good."

My nostrils flared. I wanted to wrestle the plate right out of his hands as he picked it up. But that wouldn't be very ladylike. "Sure, enjoy." I shrugged and tried not to choke as I salivated. The hunger that gnawed at my stomach was so intense that it hurt. I knew it was the right choice to avoid the high-calorie dinner, but as I watched Max mop up the butter sauce with the chicken a wave of dizziness washed over me. I didn't think I was ever going to make it through the evening if I had to watch him eat it.

"Excuse me, I'm just going to use the restroom."

As I walked past all the other diners savoring their delicious food, I felt even worse. Was this what the next six weeks would be like? I didn't think I was going to make it.

Inside the restroom an older buxom woman sat on a metal folding chair. She glanced up at me with disdain when I stepped inside—apparently I'd interrupted her crossword puzzle.

"One's busted, use three."

"What about two?"

"What's wrong with three?"

"I don't know. I just didn't know why I couldn't use two if only one is broken."

"Trust me, you want to use three. It's more spacious." She winked at me.

"What is that supposed to mean?" All of my frustration that had been building up—since I'd seen those numbers on my scale—threatened to boil over.

LILLIANNA BLAKE

CHAPTER 4

The woman shook her head. "Look, lady, use whatever bathroom you want, alright?"

I frowned and pushed the door to the second stall open. As the woman had said, it was quite narrow. In fact, I had to straddle the toilet in order to get the door closed.

The only good thing was that I didn't actually have to go. I just needed to get away from all the delicious food. I sighed as I tried to get control of my emotions. All of my self-confidence seemed to disappear when I'd seen those numbers on my scale. No matter how I tried to tell myself that it would all be fine, panic caused my heart to flutter.

"You alright in there?"

"Excuse me?"

"I'm just asking."

I was mortified that she would think it was okay to talk to me while I was in such a private space. Irritated, I stood up and tried to open the door. When I did, I found that I couldn't get it open far enough for me to get out. I backed up as far as I could, but the door would not swing past my knee.

I tried to lean forward and climb over the toilet at the same time, but that only caused me to slip and nearly launch my foot into the toilet.

"So, are you still okay?" The woman's voice came from just outside the door.

"No, I guess not." I frowned. I was sure there had to be a way to get out of the bathroom stall. I just had to focus. But every way I could think of only led to me getting more frustrated. The space under the door was far too small to fit through. The walls of the stall went all the way up to the ceiling. "I can't get out!"

"Hm. I guess you wish you'd used three now, huh?" The woman chuckled.

"This isn't funny! Could you please stop laughing and get me out of here?"

"Oh, there's no way out. Do you have your pants up at least?"

I looked down at my pants. Luckily, I'd never pulled them down. "What do you mean there's no way out?"

"I mean, I'll have to get the maintenance guy to take the door off."

"Why would you let me go in here if you knew that I wouldn't be able to get back out?"

"Hey, I tried to warn you, but you wanted to get all snippy with me, so I thought I'd let you learn from your own mistakes." She laughed again.

"Please help me!"

"Alright, alright, I'll be right back with Rocco."

"Rocco." I winced.

"Sammy?" Max's voice made my body jolt. It sounded like he was right outside the bathroom door. "Are you in there? Are you okay? I just wanted to know if you wanted dessert."

My eyes filled with tears. I was stuck like a sardine inside a public restroom stall waiting for a man named Rocco to pry me out, and my fiancée was asking me if I wanted dessert.

"No. I don't want any dessert."

He must have heard the tears in my voice because he sounded more concerned when he spoke again. "Sammy, are you sick?"

"No worries, bro. She's not sick, she's stuck." The second voice sounded rough and his presence was accompanied by a strong scent of cigarette smoke.

"Stuck?" Max repeated.

"Max, please, just wait for me at the car."

"Are you sure?"

"Please, Max!" I was already embarrassed enough, I didn't want him to see me stuck in a bathroom stall.

"Don't worry, I'll have you out in a jiff." Rocco went to work on the door.

I wiped away my tears. I didn't want Max to know that I'd cried over being stuck in a bathroom, but I knew that if I'd been just a few pounds slimmer, I would have been able to squeeze my way out through that door.

"Pearl, why didn't you tell her to use the other stall?" Rocco clucked his tongue.

"I tried. She didn't want to listen."

"Bet you will next time, eh?" Rocco chuckled as he pulled the door right off the hinges.

I hurried out of the stall.

"Thank you." I couldn't quite look at him.

"No problem." He started putting the door back.

"Towel?" Pearl held out a folded-up paper towel.

I scowled at her and made my way out of the bathroom. Max was waiting for me just outside the door.

"Max I told you to meet me outside!"

"What is it with you thinking I would ever leave you stranded?" He wrapped an arm around my shoulders. "Rough night, huh?"

I nodded. I felt tears threaten my eyes again. I knew I should tell him about my weight gain so that he could understand why I was upset, but I was too embarrassed. Max never had to worry about his weight. I doubted that he could understand what I was going through.

As he drove me back to my apartment, I was quiet.

"Sammy, is everything okay with us?" He glanced over at me.

"Of course it is." I squeezed his hand.

"Are you excited?" He looked into my eyes.

"Of course I am." I smiled. "I'm over-the-moon excited."

"You don't seem very excited. I mean, yesterday yes,

but today—well, it seems like you're a little off."

"We all have our off days." It made my palms sweat to lie to him, but I didn't want to tell him the truth. How could I admit that I'd slacked off and gained back twenty pounds? He wasn't going to understand, when he'd never had to diet in his life.

"Really?" He parked the car outside my apartment. "Why do you think it's not?"

"Well, you're not telling me things." He narrowed his eyes. "It doesn't seem like you're enjoying the wedding planning."

"I am, I promise. Maybe I'm just feeling a little overwhelmed."

"You know we could get a wedding planner if that would make things easier."

"No way!" I shook my head. "I want to plan the wedding. I only get one chance." I grinned at him.

"Now this is true." He kissed me. "But I hate to see you stressed out over it."

"I'm fine, really. Like you said—it's just been a rough night."

"Alright. If you say so." He nodded, then kissed me once more. "Good night, Sammy."

"Good night, Max."

CHAPTER 5

Once I was alone in my apartment, I slumped down on my couch. My mind kept returning to the look on Gail's face. Then it shifted to Pearl and Rocco's laughter. To make matters worse, I was so hungry that my stomach was growling.

I forced myself to get up off the couch to check the fridge.

While I'd been on my weight loss journey, I'd filled the fridge with fresh fruit, vegetables, and low-calorie snacks. Now I realized that I'd allowed some bad habits to make their way back onto the shelves.

There was cream cheese to go with the bagels on the counter. There were wedges of exquisite imported cheese to pair with wine. There was even a small chocolate Easter Bunny—where had that even come from?

No wonder I'd had gained weight.

"Time for some spring cleaning." I grabbed a trash bag and began tossing out all of the tempting foods in the fridge. By the time I was done there was very little left. I knew that I might be tempted to dig into the bag, so I tied it up tight and marched it right down to the dumpster in the parking lot.

When I returned to the apartment, I was ready to eat. I opened up the fridge again to see if there was anything left. I pushed a half-empty pickle jar out of the way and found what I was looking for—celery—wilted, limp celery. I grimaced and unsheathed it from the bag.

"Back to basics."

I closed the fridge. Then I opened it and grabbed the cream cheese. "Baby steps."

With a butter knife and my spoils I walked back to the couch. As I began chowing down on the chewy celery I vowed to myself that I would go to the grocery store the next day.

I turned on the television to try to block out some of my thoughts. As I watched the images flicker across the screen, I felt just as stuck as I'd been in the bathroom stall.

I knew that I needed to get motivated to be able to lose the weight I'd gained back, but the blow was so crushing that it seemed pointless.

I decided it was time to get out of my head and get into some writing. Just as I stood up to do so, a new show started on the television.

"You! Yes, you! Isn't it time you took some responsibility? Isn't time you stopped being lazy?"

I froze at the questions.

"You're the only one putting that food in your

mouth! You're the only one letting yourself sit on that couch!"

I raised an eyebrow and looked back at the screen. A man in full army fatigues stood in the center of a gym mat.

"When you're tired of giving the same old excuse about not losing the weight, that's when you sign up for my program—guaranteed to make you lose thirty pounds in thirty days or your money back!"

He shouted so forcefully that his cheeks blazed red. "So are you going to come in and see me, or are you going to make another excuse?"

He might as well have said my name. He seemed to be talking only to me. Maybe that was what I needed. A little good old-fashioned discipline and hard work might whip me into the shape I wanted to be in for my wedding.

I turned the television off, determined that I'd stop by the gym the next day after grocery shopping.

"That's right, no more excuses. Now to get some work done."

I sat down in front of my computer, determined to immerse myself in the latest book of my *B.I.G. Girls Club* series. I read back over the inspirational words that the main character Zara shared with one of her clients.

"I am worth it." I stared at the faint reflection of my face in the computer monitor. "And so is my dream wedding."

When I opened my eyes the next morning, the first thing that struck me was hunger. It wasn't the subtle kind of hunger that would wait for me to prepare a delicious and healthy breakfast. It was the ravenous kind of hunger that took over every thought in my mind.

I crawled out of bed and made my way to the kitchen. I already knew that there was very little to eat. I'd thrown out the unhealthy foods the day before. If only I hadn't walked it down to the dumpster I could have dug through the trash for some kind of decent meal. I searched the freezer in the hope that I might have missed something. But the only thing that remained were frozen vegetables, a pack of chicken breasts, and some fish that I was sure was well past its date.

I dressed and headed out.

At one time the grocery store had been one of my favorite places to go. It was my opportunity to build a delicious menu for the week ahead. However, lately I'd been picking up more microwave meals than fresh food. I'd been so focused on the wedding that I wasn't taking the time to pre-plan meals. I thought again about the state of my wedding dress—or, more precisely, the state of my body in that beautiful wedding dress. I sighed.

Not planning healthy meals had obviously taken its toll on me.

CHAPTER 6

The doors to the grocery store slid open. I grabbed a cart and made my way inside. Despite the temptation of the cookies, hot deli items, and assorted pastries that were cleverly positioned just inside the door, I forced myself in the direction of the produce section.

In the past, all of the bright colors of the vegetables would call to me. Now when I saw a plump red tomato all I could think of was a round jelly-filled doughnut. I didn't want to go back to counting every calorie. With a pout on my lips I tossed a head of broccoli, a bag of kale, and an assortment of peppers into my basket. Resentment built within me with every vegetable I added to the pile.

I was just about done with my slim list when a woman brushed by me. Her shopping cart was filled to the brim with all kinds of goodies. There were cupcakes, potato chips, and even soda. Soda! I couldn't remember the last time soda was on my grocery list. Lust bubbled up within me. It heated me up from the inside out. The woman who pushed the cart was nowhere near overweight. She had the freedom to eat whatever she pleased and was obviously not afraid to use it.

I fixated on the shopping cart. When the poor unsuspecting woman stepped away from her cart to reach for a gallon of milk, I did the only thing I could do. I curled my hands around the handle of her cart and I took off across the grocery store with it.

"Hey! Hey, that's my cart! That woman stole my cart!"

Her screams followed me to the checkout line. In my defense, it wasn't as if her purse was in the cart, just her delicious, mouth-watering groceries. I tried to blend in with a group of people waiting to check out. Luckily the line moved fast. I started to pile the groceries on to the conveyor belt when the clerk looked at me with a condescending stare.

"Ma'am, we have a problem."

I did my best to ignore the fact that he called me ma'am.

"These are my groceries, there are no problems. I'm starving—can we hurry this up?"

He swept his eyes up and down my body. "Starving?" He shook his head. "Sorry, but this is the ten items or less line and you have way more than ten items." He pointed to the endless line that snaked out of the next aisle. "You're going to have to go over there."

I frowned. "Can't you make an exception? Just this once? I've had a really rough time—"

"There she is! That's her! She took my groceries!"

"It's not like you paid for them yet!" I cringed at the sight of the security guards. It was in that moment that I realized I'd let my hunger go right past angry to crazy.

I fled the grocery store as fast as I could. In the middle of the run to my car I gave myself a little credit for getting some cardio in. I peeled out of the parking lot just as the security officers hopped into their golf cart to chase me. My heart pounded.

Once I was safe on the road, I started to laugh at the absurdity of the situation. Never in my life had I done anything so reckless or insane. But my laughter soon faded. No matter how strange the experience in the grocery store was, I was still quite hungry.

I pulled into one of the many fast food places that lined the city street. For a moment I weighed my options. I could have something reasonably healthy, or I could indulge after my harrowing experience in the grocery store.

I decided that what I needed to do was focus on making healthier choices. At least if I was in the drive-through, there wasn't much chance of my stealing someone else's food. Unless of course I was up for a carjacking. I placed my order for oatmeal and a black coffee. When I got to the window to receive it, I cringed at the scent of the plain oatmeal.

"Do you have any sugar packets? How about some cream for the coffee? Any raisins or anything I could add to the oatmeal?"

The young man nodded and filled up a small paper bag with all of the extras I asked for. By the time I was done doctoring my breakfast, there was more sugar in it than there was oatmeal. I sighed with defeat as I spooned the oatmeal into my mouth. It tasted good, but I knew that I'd made it way less healthy than it could have been.

I remembered the commercial I'd seen on television the night before. Maybe things had gotten so bad that I needed that kind of motivation from someone who would not let me make any excuses. How else was I going to lose twenty pounds in six weeks?

After I finished my breakfast I drove toward the gym. I knew they had trainers of all different kinds there. I was sure that one of them would be able to help me.

CHAPTER 7

When I opened the door to the gym I was greeted by a burst of cold air. It always felt so nice and cool when I first walked into the gym. Once I'd gotten through a workout, however, it usually felt like a sauna. I walked up to the front desk and smiled at the perky brunette behind it.

"Hi, Marla."

"Samantha, it's been a while." She wagged her finger at me.

I willed myself not to fantasize about snapping her finger in half. Apparently the oatmeal had not taken the edge off my aggression.

"Well, you know...I've been busy planning for the wedding."

"Oh yes, congratulations." She beamed at me.

I felt better about not snapping her finger.

"About that...I was wondering—do any of your trainers specialize in a more—I don't know—*strict* form of training?"

"Strict how?" She tilted her head to the side.

"Have you seen that commercial for the drill sergeant that guarantees thirty pounds in thirty days?"

"Ah, you want to drop some weight before the wedding?" She nodded. "What bride doesn't? Let's see…I think we have someone who would be perfect for you. He doesn't come in for another twenty minutes. Why don't you hop on one of the bikes for a warm-up and as soon as he comes in, I'll send him straight over to you. But Samantha, you should know, thirty pounds in thirty days isn't realistic or healthy."

"I know." I nodded.

I decided not to ask her opinion about twenty pounds in six weeks. I walked over to one of the stationary bikes and dropped my purse on the floor beside it. I tried not to think about the incident at the grocery store.

Once I'd mounted the bike I began to relax. I actually enjoyed exercising—it was the making time for it that was the hardest part for me. I willed my mind to focus on the chapter of my book that I was working to complete. Without realizing it, I went faster and faster on the bicycle. My heart pumped. My breath grew ragged.

Suddenly, I was into it. In my mind, I was blowing down a country road with the wind in my hair. The harder I pedaled, the more I forgot that I was in the middle of a gym, not a country road. My legs pumped and pumped. I rocked back and forth on the bicycle. The world around me swayed. It wasn't until I heard a subtle creak that I realized there might be a problem.

I tried to stop pedaling but my feet were flying. I gripped the handlebars of the stationary bike and admitted to myself that it was no longer stationary. It wobbled back and forth with a dangerous tilt. I looked down to see that the bolts that held the bike into the gym floor were loose. The bike swayed hard to the right and started to fall. I reached out my hands to catch myself.

Instead, I caught a chest as thick and hard as a brick wall.

"Careful there." His deep voice drew my attention right away. I looked up into the darkest brown eyes I'd ever seen. "No injuries allowed. No excuses."

As he helped me off the bike, I took in the sight of his camouflage muscle shirt and skin-tight spandex shorts. The man defined the term fit, from the ripple of his arms to the washboard of his stomach.

"I'm Blake." He held out his hand to me. "I'll be your trainer."

I shook his hand while trying to think of a good reason for him not to be my trainer. The truth was, just the look of him scared me. How could he understand what it was like to be a bigger person?

"I'm Samantha. But you know, I think maybe——"

"No thinking. From now on, I will think for you." He jabbed me in the forehead with his forefinger. "This belongs to me now."

"Uh, my head?"

"Yes, and everything that's in it. You don't need a brain to train—that's my motto!"

I stared at him. "I think that's the oddest motto I've ever heard."

"What did I tell you about thinking?" He jabbed my forehead again.

"Stop it!" I swatted at his hand.

He grabbed the whistle that hung around his neck and blew loud and hard on it until I had to cover my ears.

"Drop and give me twenty!"

"Twenty? You know, I think this was a mistake. I'll just be going—"

"Going to look like a whale in that wedding dress!"

"Excuse me?" I turned back to look at him.

"That's right, you heard me. I'm not here to make you feel pretty, Samantha, I'm here to make you look gorgeous in that dress. Isn't that what you want?"

I bit into my bottom lip. It was what I wanted—more than anything. "Yes, but you don't have to be rude about it."

"You're not going to cry, are you?" He sneered at me. "If you're going to cry, it'll be another twenty."

I scowled at him. He blew the whistle hard again and pointed to the floor. I couldn't remember a time when I'd wanted to punch someone as much as I wanted to punch this man. But I also wanted him to make me look gorgeous in my wedding dress.

With a frown, I crouched down on the floor. The

thing about gym carpets is that they are scratchy and dirty. No matter how many times they are vacuumed they remained a sweat-soaked sneaker-soiled desert. Still, I put my hands down and stretched out my legs.

CHAPTER 8

As I started doing push-ups, Blake counted above me.

"One—straighten those arms. Two—who told you to bend your knees? Two—that one didn't come close to counting. Are you doing a push-up or are you taking a nap?"

I wasn't accustomed to this kind of motivation. In fact, I'd spent the past year of my life building up my confidence and learning how to treat myself with kindness and love.

Blake, apparently, was not as kind.

"Lift up your butt! Lift it! Lift it!"

I had my butt precariously high in the air when it began to vibrate. With my muscles strained to the max and my body already shaking, the vibration was not helpful. I wobbled and nearly fell.

"Head in the game, Samantha! Head in the game!"

I ducked before he could poke me in the forehead again. Then I remembered why the phone in my pocket was vibrating. I had set an alarm to remind me about the meeting I had at the chapel. It was to finalize the location of the wedding.

"Oh no!" I looked at my watch. "I was supposed to be at the chapel by three. I completely forgot!"

"Did anyone tell you to stop doing push-ups?"

"I'm sorry, but I've missed an appointment. I have to make a call."

"You'll make a call when I say you can make a call! Do you think that muffin top is going to lose itself? Why aren't you sweating, Samantha?"

I wiped his spit off my forehead. It was mixed with quite a bit of sweat. I wondered if he might be blind.

"Listen, Blake." I stood up, trying to make myself taller so that I could look him straight in the eye. "I appreciate your enthusiasm, but along with getting in shape, I also do have a wedding to plan."

"Your wedding isn't going to be what you want if you don't lose the weight." Blake crossed his massive arms. "You can either continue your push-ups, or you can walk out that door. If you walk out that door, you're going to have to find another trainer."

"Well, I think—" When he raised his finger to poke me in the forehead again, I ducked and dodged. "That might be for the best." I shook my head as I walked out the gym.

Maybe I needed more discipline in my life, but Blake wasn't going to be the one to give it to me. There was a big difference between motivation and being flat-out rude.

I left the gym behind and rushed to call the caretaker of the chapel. On the third ring she answered.

"Hi, this is Samantha. I had an appointment with you at three. I'm sorry, I know I'm late."

"Oh, it's no problem. I just gave your reservation to the nice couple that stopped in during your appointment time."

"Oh, that's so funny." I laughed.

"I wasn't joking."

"What?" I gripped the phone so tightly I might have broken it if it didn't already have a shatterproof case. "Please tell me you're joking."

"No, I'm sorry. The chapel is in high demand and you didn't call to say that you'd be late. I just assumed that perhaps things didn't go well and you wouldn't need the chapel after all."

"No! This can't be happening! My wedding is in two months. There's no time to get another venue!"

"I'm terribly sorry, but these things happen. Perhaps you could have a nice beach wedding?"

"But I get sunburn!" I wailed into the phone. "Hello? Hello?" I was met with the sound of the dial tone.

I stood beside my car and tried not to burst into tears. Just when I thought everything was going to be perfect, it was all falling apart. I didn't fit into my dress, Max wouldn't tell me his plans for the honeymoon, and now I had lost the wedding venue.

How was I going to explain to Max that I just didn't show up for the meeting? Would there even still be a wedding?

As if he could sense my distress, my phone began to ring. I saw that it was Max calling. I couldn't bring myself to answer it. I needed time to fix everything that had gone wrong.

I drove away from the gym with tears in my eyes. I still had no food and twenty pounds to lose. I found myself parked in front of Stephanie's house. I didn't even think about where I was going. When I opened my car door she opened the front door of her house and stepped outside.

"Samantha? I didn't know you were coming over!"

"Oh, Stephanie, I've ruined everything!" The tears flowed hot and sticky against my cheeks.

"Samantha!" She wrapped her arms around me in a tight hug. "Don't you worry about a thing, we'll figure it all out. Come inside. You probably just need something to eat."

I muffled my moan against her shoulder. What I wanted was an entire wedding cake to devour, but I knew I couldn't risk gaining another pound.

Stephanie steered me inside. Through my gulps and hiccups she managed to hear the whole story of the disaster I'd caused.

"So we need to find a new place for the wedding. That shouldn't be too hard. Just take a deep breath.

Weddings do this to people. It's supposed to be the happiest time of our lives, but for many people, I think it ends up being the most stressful."

I grabbed a handful of tissues from the box she held out. As I wiped at my eyes she patted my other hand. "I know what you need—a wedding planner."

"But I wanted to do it myself!" I frowned.

"I know you did, but you still will. The best part about a wedding planner is that they use your ideas and do all of the work to make sure that your day is perfect. That will give you the time you need to focus on losing weight."

"That does sound good." I sighed. "As long as he or she will listen to exactly what I want."

"I'm sure he will. A friend of mine got married last year and she said she had the most amazing wedding planner. I can get his name for you if you'd like."

"I guess." I frowned. "You don't think I'm giving up?"

"No, sweetie. I think you're delegating. You're churning out books like crazy, you have your blog that you're working on all of the time, and now you've set a weight loss goal for yourself. If you don't do something to take the pressure off you soon, you're going to crack."

"You're right, you're right." I nodded. "Alright, I'll give it a shot."

"I'll e-mail you his information."

"Okay." I took a deep breath and smoothed my

palms down over my knees. "Thanks, Stephanie. I'm going to go home and get my head on straight."

CHAPTER 9

I turned on my music as soon as I walked in the door of my apartment. I needed more than just computer time. I needed to soothe my nerves and free my spirit.

As I danced around the living room I decided this was much better than working out with Blake.

After about twenty minutes of dancing, I headed over to my computer. Ever since I'd started my blog, I found it useful for my writing, but also for accountability. Whenever I set a new goal for myself, I'd update my blog so that my readers would be able to hold me to it.

I needed to do something important. I needed to admit to my readers that I'd put some weight back on. I was hopeful that I'd gain support from them to help me to lose the weight before my wedding.

As I typed out the blog post, the truth poured out of me. It wasn't about the bad food choices I'd made, or the fact that I'd neglected going to yoga and my regular meditation class—it was about much more than that. It was about losing myself in the planning of the wedding.

My quest for perfection had caused me to lose my sense of self.

After I posted the entry, I thought about it for a long time. Was it really so bad that the chapel fell through? The only reason I'd chosen it was because it seemed like the right place. But was that where I really wanted to get married?

Sure, I planned my wedding from the time I was a little girl, but I wasn't that little girl any more. My tastes had changed as I'd grown up.

I saw that I had an e-mail from Stephanie with the wedding planner's information. If I was going to let someone else plan my wedding, I needed to figure out what I actually wanted. I closed my eyes and tried to picture the big day. Was it inside? Was it outside?

There were two things that I knew had to be part of my wedding. Max—and me twenty pounds lighter.

I sighed as my mind returned to my weight gain. The trainer had been a bust, but I still needed to focus on fixing the problem.

I did a quick search for diets that would help me to lose weight fast. As I expected, the results were numerous. I waded through any that required a pill or a machine. Then I cross-checked the results that remained with warnings of sudden death, sexual dysfunction, and abnormal hair growth. I chose the top ten of the diets that remained.

The first not only seemed doable, but it sounded fun.

All I had to do was juice pineapple for five days and I was guaranteed to lose ten pounds. Ten wasn't everything I wanted to lose, but it would be a good start, and I would still have five weeks left. I added the diet to my blog so that my readers would know what I was up to. A surge of excitement rushed through me as my heart pounded. I was sure that I would have everything under control by the next day.

After a long shower I called Max to wish him goodnight.

"Hey, babe, are you feeling any better?"

"Yes. I'm sorry I've been a little crazy lately. I think you were right. I decided to get a wedding planner after all."

"Great! I hope that means we'll get to spend a little more time together. I've been missing you."

"I'm sorry, Max. You know how busy I've been with all of the books and the blog. I really wish that you would just quit your job and come run my tech for me."

"Run your tech?" He laughed a little. "Sammy, you know I can't just quit my job."

"Why can't you? Don't you think it would be fun to work together?"

"Maybe."

I noticed the distance in his voice. "It doesn't sound like a good idea to you?"

"Sure it does, but we just have so much on our plate right now—with the wedding and then the move."

I cringed at the mention of the move. It was going to be hard for me to leave behind the apartment that I'd lived in since college. Max owned his own house so it made the most sense to move in with him. But I hadn't really given a lot of thought to what it might mean to be giving up the solace I often enjoyed.

"There's always going to be stuff on our plate, Max. We have to be brave enough to try anyway." I frowned. I thought he and I were on the same page about our future. "I thought it would be amazing if we worked together. We could travel whenever we wanted and if we have kids—"

"*If* we have kids?"

Max's voice sounded tense.

I swallowed hard. "When we have kids, we'll both be available to them. What could be better than that?"

"It sounds ideal, Sammy. It's just that I don't want to put any undue pressure on our marriage when it's just starting off. I'm not saying no, I'm just saying let's think it through and make sure that it's right for us."

I sighed. Sometimes I wondered why I couldn't just tweak Max's brain and make him agree with me. As much as I hated to admit it, he did have a point.

"Alright, you're right. We do have a lot to focus on right now with the wedding."

"Great. Don't forget about your bridal shower."

"And your bachelor party. How many strippers are you going to have?"

"Oh wow, are you volunteering? I don't know how I feel about you getting naked around my friends."

"Max!"

He laughed. I loved the sound of his laugh, even if he managed to infuriate me.

"Sammy, when are you going to get it through your head that the only woman I ever want naked and twirling around a pole is you?"

I raised an eyebrow and considered how to respond to that. "Well I did take that pole dancing class."

"Fine, so no strippers at the bachelor party, and I'll make sure that we get a stripper pole in the honeymoon suite."

"Ugh, what kind of hotel offers that? You're not planning to get one of those rooms with a heart-shaped tub, are you? And magic fingers in the bed?"

"Oh trust me sweetheart, there are going to be magic fingers—"

"Max!"

"I'm sorry." He laughed again. Then his laughter stopped. "Wait a minute, you're not planning to have a stripper at your bridal shower, are you? Don't women do that now?"

"I don't know; Stephanie is planning it." I smiled a little at the hint of jealousy in his voice. "Would that bother you?"

"Huh."

"Would it?"

"I guess that depends."

"On what?"

"On whether or not you want to see me in a Speedo, because I'm the only stripper giving you a lap dance."

"Oh, is that so?"

"Yes, ma'am, and to be honest I'm not a fan of Speedos. They chafe."

"And you know this how?" I laughed.

"Never mind about that."

"I bet. I love you, Max."

"I love you too. I'd probably make a sexy cop though. With the sunglasses and the handcuffs."

"Hm. I'll run it by Stephanie."

"You'd better not!"

"Bye, Max! Love you!" I hung up before he could sputter out everything he had to say.

I was in a much better mood after I talked to Max. He always brightened my day. Plus the thought of him in sunglasses, a Speedo, and armed with handcuffs was rather pleasant. I was more determined than ever to look amazing for him when I walked down the aisle.

CHAPTER 10

I was faced with the task of having to find a new grocery store. I could only hope that no one had taken a picture of me during my stolen shopping cart escapade and shared it with other grocery stores in the area.

I was excited to start my pineapple juice diet. The instructions were very specific. Buy fresh pineapple, juice fresh pineapple, and drink fresh pineapple juice. It sounded delicious and healthy.

When I walked into the grocery store I was relieved to see that it wasn't very crowded. In the produce section there was a small display of pineapples available.

"Don't they look cheerful!" I smiled. I went to pick up one of the pineapples. One of the spikes on it pricked my palm. "Ouch! Stupid pineapple." I tossed it in my cart. I had no idea how many pineapples I would need. How much juice would one pineapple yield? I shrugged and tossed ten into the grocery cart. "That should be enough to get me started."

As I wheeled the cart to the register I noticed a few

looks from employees and others in the store. I guess not everyone was informed about the pineapple diet.

Carefully I loaded each pineapple up onto the conveyor belt. The cashier was busy talking to the previous customer. He absentmindedly pushed the button to move the conveyor belt forward.

When he did, all of the pineapples began to fall over. It was a bit like dominoes the way they knocked into one another.

"No, oh stop!" I tried to catch a few of the pineapples but their sharp spikes made me shriek.

"What's going on here? Did you knock those pineapples over? Why would you do that?" The cashier ran out to stop the pineapples, but they rolled away. Other customers jumped and dodged them. Suddenly the PA system screeched on.

"Please be advised there are pineapples rolling down the aisles. Please exercise caution, our staff and security team are working hard to fix the problem."

In that moment, as I watched a security officer walk toward me, I was pretty sure that I was never going to be able to grocery shop again.

"Ma'am, ma'am, you know you're going to have to pay for those pineapples."

"If one more person calls me ma'am…" I frowned. "Don't worry, I want the pineapples. It wasn't my fault they rolled away."

"Sure. Just pay the man, and take your pineapples."

I sighed and paid for the pineapples. As I carried my bags to the car I hoped that the juicing would be more successful than the purchasing. Then it struck me. Could you even juice a pineapple? I'd certainly never juiced one before.

When I got back to my apartment I pulled out my juicer. I had to look up a video to figure out just the right way to cut and juice pineapple. Once it was juiced I drank it down. It was a sharper taste than I expected. It made my tongue burn and my cheeks tingle. But it also gave me an energy boost. With a positive attitude and a rush, I dialed the number for the wedding planner. It only rang twice before he answered.

"Let me plan your destiny, this is Will speaking. Will you be happy? Will you get everything you've ever dreamed about? Will you dance with joy? Oh yes, you will, with Will!"

I blinked at the rapid words that flooded my ear. "Okay. Do you do weddings?"

"Yes I do, yes I will."

I cringed. I wasn't sure that I could work with someone who had a catch phrase.

"It's in two months."

"Oh, two months?" He cleared his throat. "Sure, I can do that."

"Can we meet today?"

"Shall we share lunch?"

I started to agree and then I remembered that the

only thing I would be consuming was pineapple. "No, not for lunch. Can you meet me at my apartment, or do you have an office?"

"Your apartment will be fine. Just text me your address, I'm available whenever you want me to come."

"Great." I smiled with relief. Between the pineapple buzz and Will's enthusiasm I started to think that my day might be improving.

CHAPTER 11

I spent the morning cleaning up my apartment just in case Will was the judgmental type. When I heard him ring the doorbell I wondered if I'd made a mistake. Could anyone else really plan my wedding? I opened the door to find the strangest man I'd ever laid eyes on.

"Well, aren't you just a peach?" He winked his long dark lashes at me.

They had to be fake—no one's eyelashes curled like that. He also wore a very heavy amount of eyeliner. His black hair was spiked and tipped with neon green dye. His clothes looked like something out of a comic book. He wore a deep plum button-down shirt with skin-tight black pants, although they could have been stockings for all of how thin and tight they were.

"Will?"

"Yes. I'm Will." He grinned. "Now let's have a look around your place so I can get an idea of your taste."

"Wait, I—uh—"

He brushed right past me and into the apartment. I

tried to think of an excuse to boot him right back out the door. He certainly wasn't going to be able to plan my wedding.

"Lovely—uh-huh, interesting." He stopped short in the middle of the living room. "Well, well, Samantha, I know quite a bit about you now."

"That's impossible." I looked around my apartment. I'd already packed quite a bit of my personal items. The walls were fairly bare and even my bookshelves were empty. What could he know? "I don't think that this is going to work out. I think you should go."

"Let's make a deal." Will rubbed his hands together.

"A deal? Maybe you didn't hear me?" I raised an eyebrow.

"I heard you just fine. If I can't tell you more about you than some of your friends can, then I'll walk right out that door. Okay?"

"Okay." I frowned. He wouldn't be able to tell me anything; I was a little bothered by the waste of time.

"Samantha, you are an amazing young woman who has waited for just the right man to come into her life."

"I'm sure that's true of every bride you meet."

"You'd be surprised." He laughed. "But I'm not done. It's very important to you to be honest. You have a doting mother who wants nothing more than to see you married. Your best friend is the man you're marrying, although you probably have one or two more good friends. Otherwise, you're not terribly social. You've never been in a fistfight and you are a writer."

I narrowed my eyes. I had to admit that he was right about everything he'd said. Sure, some could be good guesses, but I was intrigued.

"You could have just looked up my name to find out I'm a writer. You could have picked up a lot of things about me if you came across my blog."

"Oh, a blog, hm? I guess I'll have to become one of your followers. But I'm betting that none of them would reveal to me that you have been waiting for this day to happen for years. I don't have to be a psychic to know that you are one half of a fairytale romance. I can make your wedding the perfect backdrop for that romance. What do you think?" He smiled.

I tilted my head from one side to the other. "I'm not sure. I'm sorry. I just don't know if our styles would really mesh."

"I understand, I do." He made his way into the kitchen. "I just ask that you open your mind to all of the possibilities. You only get one wedding—at least we hope, right?" He laughed. "So you want to be able to enjoy it."

I sighed. Between the weight issue and my writing, I hadn't really been enjoying the planning of my wedding all that much. Will had a point. With his help, I might just be able to have the wedding I hoped for—a wedding that, as of now, I didn't even have a location for.

"Oh, are you doing the pineapple cleanse? Here, let

me whip that up for you while you and I discuss." He waved me right out of my own kitchen.

I took a seat at the bar and watched as he easily diced the pineapple and tossed it into the juicer.

"My cousin did this and lost thirty pounds in about two months. Is your weight an issue?" He tilted his head back and forth as if he was trying to decide for himself.

CHAPTER 12

Was my weight an issue? The question made my head feel like it was going to explode. I wanted to tell him just how much of an issue it was and how it had been an issue for so long that I didn't have any other issues. But I still wasn't sure if he was the right choice for a wedding planner.

"I could stand to lose some before the wedding."

"Hm. Every bride is beautiful, you know." He winked at me.

"Sure. I know. But there's a comfortable place I'd like to be."

"I understand. Now this just needs a little something." He wiggled through the kitchen. He opened and closed every cabinet and drawer until he found what he was looking for. He moved so fast that I didn't even see what he'd selected, but whatever it was, he sprinkled it onto the top of my drink.

"Thanks." I took a sip. "Wow, this is better than I expected!"

"Exactly, Samantha—and if you work with me, that's what you'll be saying every single day. Yes, you will!"

I cringed at the "will" reference again but tried to keep an open mind. He was quite perceptive, he'd figured out how to use my juicer a lot faster than I ever could, and his enthusiasm was something to be admired.

"Alright, Will, let's give it a try." I smiled. "I am in a bit of a mess. The wedding is in two months and I now have no location."

"What kind of location were you interested in?" Will whipped out his phone.

"I had my heart set on this little chapel."

"Religious then?"

"Not exactly. I just liked the building."

"What did you like about the building?"

"I suppose just how airy it is. It has large windows and high ceilings."

"So you like the feeling of being outside?" Will looked up from his phone.

"Yes, I guess." I nodded and sipped my drink.

"Well, then why not have the ceremony outside?" Will clapped his hands. "I have the perfect place."

"I don't know. Bugs. Bugs. Sunburn. Bugs." I scrunched up my nose. "What if there's a bird poop disaster?"

Will laughed. "I see you like to think of every potential problem. That's a good quality. But you must trust me. I always have the perfect solution. Just come see the place with me? I'm sure you'll enjoy your visit."

"Okay. I guess it wouldn't hurt to check it out."

"Great! I will set up the appointment, yes I will." He saluted me and walked toward the door. "You will be so happy with your wedding, yes you will!" He let himself out of the apartment.

I stared after him.

"I hope I will." I snapped my fingers. "Now I'm doing it!"

By dinnertime that night, my stomach ached.

"This is normal. It's all part of the process. Just have to get through a few hours of hunger and I'll be fine." I turned on the television to try to distract myself. As I watched, a commercial for a steakhouse came on.

"Sink your teeth into it. Go on, you know that you want to. Just take a bite of this juicy goodness."

I did want to take a bite. In fact, I wanted to devour it. I groaned and changed the channel. On the next one was a movie. The stars sat at a table in a fine restaurant. As I watched, they were delivered plates of pasta soaked in sauce and dotted with meatballs.

"That's it!" I turned the television off and retreated to my computer. Television was far too dangerous for me to be involved in right now.

I tried working on my book, but when my fingertips struck the keys they made a subtle crunching sound that reminded me of munching on potato chips. I didn't realize I'd started drooling until a splash hit the keyboard.

"Oh, this is not working." I shook my head.

I turned off the computer and paced back and forth. I remembered that sometimes the best way to get through the detox of a diet change was to sweat it out. "Yoga. That's what I need—something peaceful that can take my mind off my hunger and give my body a chance to sweat it out while the pineapple juice works its magic." I called my usual yoga studio.

"Hi, it's Bonnie." She sounded so happy to answer the phone that I couldn't help but smile.

"Hi, Bonnie, my name is Samantha. I've taken your class before and I was just wondering if you had any classes tomorrow?"

"Actually we do. There's one at ten. Do you think you could make it?"

"Sure, that sounds perfect."

"Oh, that's so great, Samantha. I can't wait to see you."

I was sure that she didn't remember me, but that didn't change the fact that it perked me up to be treated so well.

I used the motivation of the upcoming yoga class to get me through most of my evening. When that began to fade, I logged onto my blog. I saw that I had quite a few comments from my readers.

SWF, why would you put yourself through the pineapple

cleanse?

SWF, aren't you concerned about your overall health? Are you sure this is safe?

I bit into my bottom lip. It warmed my heart to know that they cared, but it also bothered me that they thought it was a mistake. I looked up some of the reviews I'd read about the pineapple cleanse and posted them for my readers. I also added a note to thank them for their concern. I promised to keep them updated and mentioned the yoga class as a way I was balancing the cleanse with physical activity. I sat back in my chair and thought about what they'd said.

Was I taking this need to get the twenty pounds off fast a little too far? I didn't think so. Lots of people went on crash diets when they needed to drop weight. Celebrities, athletes, models, and of course, brides.

I turned my focus from my blog to my book. I added in a section about motivation and how it comes in all forms.

"Sometimes it's about self-discipline." I cringed at the memory of Blake, hoping I was settling into the right kind of discipline for me.

CHAPTER 13

When I woke up the next morning, I felt an urge deep within me that I'd never experienced before. I likened it to the drive that supernatural bloodsuckers felt when waking from a one-hundred-year slumber. My entire body yearned for food.

I sat up and was hit by a wave of dizziness.

"Ugh. This is not good." I rushed into the kitchen. Luckily, I couldn't devour everything in my cupboards, because I had no other food but pineapple. Unfortunately preparing the pineapple juice was a long process. By the time the whir of the juicer greeted my ears, I felt very faint. I gulped down the juice. It hit my stomach and caused a bubbly sensation.

I leaned back against the counter and sighed. I expected to be satisfied by the juice—all of the reviews had led me to believe that I would be—but I felt just as hungry.

I closed my eyes tight. "You can do this, Samantha. You can do this. Just remember the dress. Remember your goal. It's only a few more days, and you will have a jump-start on your weight loss—and you will be able to stop talking to yourself."

I rubbed my stomach and pretended that I was full. I thought maybe if I convinced my mind that I was satiated, my body would agree.

I changed into my yoga leotard and tights. The constriction reminded me of the pounds that I had put on. "Yes, I can do this." I chanted those words as I drove to the yoga studio.

Still, I was sluggish when I walked through the door. Bonnie bounced right over to me.

"Oh hi, you must be Samantha. We talked on the phone yesterday."

"Yes." I nodded. "Actually, I've taken your class before."

"I thought so, but you look different." She tilted her head to the side and studied me.

It made me feel uneasy to think that she might be analyzing every part of my body.

"I've put on a little weight."

"Oh, don't worry about that." She patted my shoulder. "This class will get rid of those extra pounds real fast."

"Not fast enough." I muttered my words under my breath. Yoga was a great exercise, but I needed speedy results.

I tasted a bit of pineapple on my tongue as I walked into the classroom. There were about a dozen other women there and none of them looked anything like me. I reminded myself that everyone was there for the same reason and no one was going to judge me. The fact that my leotard gave me a wedgie with every step I took made that idea a little hard to believe.

"Alright, everyone, let's get started."

I spread my mat out between two other women.

Bonnie sat in a lotus position at the front of the class. "I'm so glad that each and every one of you is here. There is so much to be grateful for today. I want you to think about that as we relax into our first pose. Alright?"

I noticed that she smiled at each and every person in the room, which included me—right at the moment when I freed my leotard from a rather awkward place. If she noticed she kept it to herself.

I took a deep breath in and shifted my body into position. My muscles burned and then relaxed with the stretch. I took another deep breath in. To me yoga had a smell. It was sweat, skin, and incense—even if there wasn't any burning. Some of the people wore oils on their skin or used fragrant shampoo.

Everything smelled delicious. It didn't matter that the smells weren't food smells. I still salivated like a thirsty bulldog.

"Samantha? Are you okay?" A warm hand settled on my back. I recognized the touch right away.

"I'm fine, Bonnie. I'm sorry, I'm just a little distracted."

"Just breathe deep, Samantha." Bonnie smiled.

I tried to smile back, but she smelled like vanilla ice cream. I had to fight the urge to lick her. I didn't think that would be appropriate yoga class behavior.

I tried to breathe.

"Okay, everyone, let's just have a little quiet time. Everyone calm and quiet—and deep, deep, breaths."

I stretched out on my mat. I was afraid I might fall asleep. I was exhausted. I hadn't gotten that burst of energy since the first pineapple juice I'd guzzled. I forgot to be careful and gulped down a big breath of air. All of the scents in the room combined.

The silent room was suddenly filled with a deep terrifying growl. The women on either side of me jumped off their mats with widened eyes. That was when I recognized that terrible sound had emerged from my leotard-clad stomach.

"Oh no!" I sat up. Another rumble escaped. More perfectly shaped women scattered for cover. "Wait, it's just that I'm hungry. It's not gas, it's not gas!" I tried to get to my feet but my muscles were a little sore from being out of practice and I lost my balance on the way up. I fell back down on to my mat. Another loud noise escaped.

"Okay, that was gas."

The last of the women snatched up their mats and ran. At the front of the room, Bonnie was still stretched out on her mat. She cleared her throat.

"Okay." She sat up. "I'm just going to open a window. Everyone keep relaxing." She paused on the way to the window. "Wait, where did everyone go?"

"I—uh—well, I think they thought you were sleeping. There was this weird snoring sound." I scrambled to my feet and rolled up my mat.

"Maybe it was that awful smell." Bonnie shook her head and slid the window open. "Someone had too much pineapple!"

I ran from the room with little pellet toots escaping me along the way.

Pineapple juicing had to stop!

CHAPTER 14

After yoga class I was so embarrassed that I hid out at home. I sent a text to Will to cancel our meeting and camped out in the middle of my bed. If I'd had any food other than pineapple in my apartment I would have chowed down. Instead, I used my phone to search for another diet. This time I wanted one where I wouldn't be starving. Liquid sustenance was not enough for me. My teeth longed to crunch and chew. I found one in particular that sounded too good to be true, but the results were very promising.

As I was reading about it there was a knock on the door. Then the door swung open.

"Max?"

"It's me, babe." I heard the door close.

"I'm in the bedroom."

"Oh yeah? Is everything okay?" He plopped down on the bed beside me.

"Yes, why?"

"Well, you're in Camp Bed."

"Camp Bed?" I laughed.

"Sure. Whenever you're upset about something you camp out in the middle of your bed."

I smiled at how well he knew me. "I'm okay. Really."

"Then why did I get this weird text from someone named Will?" He held up his phone and read me the text. "I will need to see you both at Cerulean Gardens in an hour. You will be there."

"Oh, he's the wedding planner. Sorry, I should have mentioned to you that I'd given him your number. I cancelled the meeting that we'd had scheduled. I guess he doesn't want it to be cancelled."

"The more important question is why do you want to cancel it?" Max wrapped an arm around my shoulders. "What's going on?"

"Oh, just a little tummy trouble."

"Want me to get you some soup?" He rubbed his hand slowly across my back. I nestled close to him and sighed.

"No, it's okay. I guess that we really should go."

"Are you sure? We could stay here and I could pamper you."

"Hm, that's tempting. But we shouldn't keep Will waiting. He's a little excitable."

"Sounds interesting."

"Let me just get changed and we can head out."

"Alright. I'll take over Camp Bed for you." He sprawled out across my bed. I laughed as I grabbed some clothes and ducked into the bathroom.

When I came back out Max held my phone in his hand. "I hope you don't mind, this looked interesting."

"I don't mind." I sat down beside him. "I'm thinking of trying it."

"So the theory here is that you eat twelve times a day?" Max laughed. "That sounds a little backwards."

"It's meant to keep my metabolism active, so that my body never stores fat." I smiled. "I really think that it's going to work."

"Sammy, you know that I support you no matter what you do. I just want you to remember that you're gorgeous. You don't need to focus on your weight."

"I know, I know. You're amazing, Max." I kissed his cheek. "But this isn't really about you. I set a goal for myself and I want to accomplish it."

"Okay." He grinned. "I guess you'd better go shopping. I went to get a drink and the only thing you have in that fridge is pineapples. Why is that anyway? Please tell me it has nothing to do with the bridal shower."

"What?" I laughed. "No. Don't worry about that. I'll go shopping this afternoon."

"Well, we can just stop on the way to the chapel. It's right around the corner."

"Oh, actually I can't go to that store any more."

"Why?" Max raised his eyebrows.

"Oh—uh—I just don't like it any more."

"I feel like there's a story there." Max studied me.

"Oh, and about the chapel—we're not going to be using it."

"What do you mean we're not going to be using it?" He took a step back and looked at me. "What's going on?"

"Well, unfortunately the chapel fell through. But there's nothing to worry about. Will has it all under control."

"Excitable Will?"

"He's unique, but he's a good wedding planner. Wait until you meet him." I grinned.

"I'm looking forward to it. But now I'm wondering if I should be."

"You should." I hugged him around the waist. "So today we're going to look at a venue he suggested. I know we were thinking indoor all the way, but now I'm wondering if it wouldn't be more fun to do something outside. I mean we could still have the reception inside. What do you think?"

"I think anywhere that I'm marrying you is going to be the most beautiful place on earth."

"Oh that gets a kiss." I laughed and planted a big kiss on his lips.

As we drove to Cerulean Gardens, I set up a series of alarms on my phone to remind myself to eat. I was a little hesitant about eating so often, but at least I wouldn't be hungry.

"Do you mind if we pick up some snacks?"

"No problem. Like I said, the grocery store—"

"Can't go there." I smiled at him. "And I'm still not telling you why."

"Hm, secrets aren't good, Sammy. Maybe I'll have to find a way to get the truth out of you."

"I might enjoy that." I laughed.

Max drove past a gas station.

"Max, I said I wanted some snacks."

"Okay, well, there's another store a few miles up."

"But I'm hungry now."

"You can't wait a few minutes?"

I fixed him with a stare that made my own eyes burn. "Max, I'm hungry." At least, that's what I thought I said, but what actually came out was: "Max, if you don't turn this car around and go back to that gas station right this second I will make sure you never drive again."

CHAPTER 15

Max stepped on the brake and looked over at me with wide eyes. "Sammy? Are you serious?"

"What?" I blinked.

"Wow." He shook his head and turned the car around. His lips were tense and his eyes narrowed. I realized I might have struck a nerve.

"Oh no, don't let that person go—Max, you should have turned!"

"Sammy, stop. I'm not going to cut in front of someone to get you some beef jerky!"

"You would if you loved me!"

Max raised both of his eyebrows. He looked at me with a half-open mouth. Then he gunned the engine right into the gas station parking lot.

"Aren't you coming in?"

"No thanks, I'll stay right here. I wouldn't want to risk not being able to drive again." He shot me a look with furrowed brows.

"I said I needed snacks." I shook my head. I had no idea why he was being so testy.

I opened the door to the gas station and was slapped in the face by the scent of grilled hot dogs, slushies, and an assortment of spices. I grabbed chips, crackers, and a small pack of cookies. Then I saw the packages of beef jerky.

They set off a sarcastic thought: "Thanks a lot, Max."

To top off my snacks, I got a bottle of water—at least that was healthy, plus it wouldn't taste like pineapple.

I piled my goods onto the counter. The man behind the counter was on the phone. I waited for a minute. He was still on the phone. I stared at the bag of chips. It wanted me to open it. It called out to me. I looked up at the man behind the counter. He was still on the phone. I snatched up the bag of chips and started to open it. The rustling alerted the man finally.

"Hey, you have to pay for that before you eat it!"

"Well, then ring me up!" I shouted. I didn't normally shout. But the situation called for it.

"There's no need to be rude."

"There's no need to ignore a paying customer who needs her snacks!" I reached into my purse to find that my wallet wasn't there. I winced when I remembered leaving it at home on the hall table.

"Well, are you going to pay or not?"

"Uh, I just have to get my boyfriend. I forgot my wallet."

"You already opened the chips!"

"He's right outside. I just have to get him."

"Like I'm going to fall for that!" He shook his head. "I'm calling the police!"

"But I didn't even eat any! I probably have enough change."

"Too late." He started dialing the phone.

All my anger melted into tears. I was going to go to jail for stealing potato chips. How would that look on my blog?

"Please, please don't call the police. He's right outside."

"Sammy? What's going on?" Max stepped through the door. "What's taking so long?"

"He's going to have me arrested!" I wailed my words.

Max's eyes widened. "What? What for?"

"She doesn't have money to pay and she opened the merchandise!"

"I forgot my wallet." I wiped at my eyes.

"Oh, Sammy." Max wrapped his arm around me. "I have money. How much is it?"

"It's too late."

"It's not too late." Max glared at him. "How much is it?"

"Eight-fifty."

"Here is ten—for your trouble."

"Oh, big spender!" The clerk rolled his eyes.

Max snatched up the snacks and steered me out of the gas station. "What is going on with you, Sammy?"

"I'm sorry." I shoved some chips into my mouth. "I

was just so hungry. I think I was a little emotional."

"A little?" He tilted his head to the side.

The alarm on my phone sounded.

"Oh good, it's time to eat!"

Max shook his head and opened my door for me.

"I'm sorry, I forgot to ask if you wanted anything. Beef jerky?" I held out the package to him.

"No thanks." He started the car.

I chowed down on as many snacks as I could for the remainder of the drive. It wasn't until we reached Cerulean Gardens that I remembered the twelve meals a day were only supposed to be one hundred and fifty calories each. I winced and tried not to think about it.

"Better?" Max looked over at me.

I nodded. "I'm sorry I acted crazy."

"No problem." He kissed me. "Mm, salty."

I laughed. "Hey, at least I'm not in handcuffs."

"Thanks to me."

"Yes, yes—my hero."

He grinned back at me.

We walked up to the front entrance, a wrought iron gate. A woman waited to greet us.

"Welcome to Cerulean Gardens." The woman before us wore a long flowing dress. Her red curls were spotted with real white flower blossoms. I was impressed with her style, but more so with the gardens that stretched out behind her. In the middle of the city, it was hard to find a natural oasis. Cerulean Gardens appeared to be one.

"This place is amazing. How did I not know it was here?"

"We only recently opened it to the public. Up until last year, we only hosted private parties and field trips."

"Why did you open up to the public now?" Max swept his gaze over the surroundings.

"We needed the income. We always intended to open to the public, but we wanted to make sure that the gardens were sturdy enough to hold up to more visitors. Luckily, we had this amazing—oh, look there he is now." She waved to a man who walked toward us.

When I caught sight of him I had to bite my tongue to keep from gasping. His dark wavy hair glinted in the sunlight. His deeply tanned skin was streaked with dirt, which only made his eyes brighter. He wore a sleeveless t-shirt that showed off his well-developed arms. As he waved back to the woman, he looked right into my eyes. I stumbled a little and leaned against Max's arm.

"Sammy, are you okay? I knew that diet was no good." Max whispered into my ear.

LILLIANNA BLAKE

CHAPTER 16

I looked into the eyes of my soon-to-be-husband and gulped back a wave of guilt. Had I really just lusted after a stranger with Max by my side?

"I'm fine, I'm fine." I smiled and gave his arm a squeeze.

I did my best not to look at the man who'd paused in front of me.

"Arielle." He nodded to the woman.

"This is Stephen." Arielle smiled. "He's our miracle worker."

"I don't know if I'd say that." Stephen lowered his eyes. His cheeks reddened. "I just love to garden."

"And it shows. Our gardens are filled with love, which makes them the perfect place for a wedding."

"Oh, congratulations." Stephen flashed a wide smile. His teeth shimmered in the sun.

I looked at Max. I did my best not to look away from him.

"Thank you. We're so looking forward to it—so happy."

"Yes." Max smiled at me. "I have to be the luckiest man on earth."

"Yes, yes you are!" Will's bright voice chimed in as he jogged up beside us. He clapped Max hard on the back—so hard that Max was knocked a few steps forward. Since I was clinging so tightly to his arm I was jerked forward as well, right into Stephen's sweaty, perfect biceps.

"Oh no!" I jumped away from him. An alarm started going off loudly in my mind.

"Are you okay?" Stephen grabbed my hand to steady me.

"Watch it." Max cast a frown in Will's direction.

"So sorry, sometimes I don't know my own strength. I'll do better about that, I will—yes I will." He sighed.

"I'm fine." I pulled away from Stephen's grasp, the alarm still pounding through my brain.

"Are you sure? Because you're kind of beeping."

I raised an eyebrow. How could he know that? Then I realized the alarm wasn't in my head—it was my cell phone. It was time to eat again.

"Oops." I pulled my phone out.

"Sammy, do you want to tour the gardens?" Max frowned.

"Yes, let me just turn this off." I struggled with the button until the alarm turned off. "Actually, I have to run back to the car."

"Sammy, can't it wait until after we do the tour?" Max shot another wary look in Will's direction.

"It'll only take a minute. Max, you know this is important to me." I met his eyes.

"Oh no, no, love birds. No squabbles allowed. I will fix this, yes I will. Max and I need to chat anyway, so why don't you get what you need from the car and we can meet at the center of the garden?"

"No, I don't—" Max began.

"Perfect!" I smiled and pecked Max's cheek.

I needed to get away from Stephen, and I had to get my next snack before I blew my new diet. I ignored Max's pleading look and headed back to the parking lot.

As soon as I was away from Stephen, I was able to calm down. It left me a little flustered to think that he'd had such an impact on me. Maybe it had been the pineapple leaving my system. I grabbed a pack of crackers from the car and polished them off.

As I turned to walk back to the entrance I saw that Arielle, Will, and Max were gone. I walked through the entrance and looked around for them. The high bushes that separated the gardens made it difficult to see anyone.

I decided to just walk toward the center, but after about ten minutes I seemed to have lost track of which path it was that would lead me there. The gardens were much larger than I'd expected them to be.

I couldn't help but notice that the garden truly was beautiful. The lush green leaves were speckled with large colorful blossoms. Butterflies danced between the different flowers. As my gaze followed the butterflies, I caught sight of Stephen's dark wavy hair.

My heart jolted. Instantly I thought I should turn around and walk the other way. But it was too late. Stephen had spotted me.

"Hi there. Are you lost?"

"Uh, I got turned around, I think." I did my best not to look at him. Instead I looked around at the foliage. I noticed that the flowers gave way to fruits and vegetables.

"Is this your garden?"

"Yes, it is. I keep the grounds here and in exchange, they allow me to use a large space to grow vegetables. I also offer classes to the locals in the area."

"Wow, that's amazing. I've never been able to keep much alive."

"Oh, that's nonsense." He waved his hand in the air. "You just have to learn a few rules of gardening and you can grow just about anything."

"I don't know. I've never been able to do it." I frowned.

"Then maybe you just haven't had the right teacher. Why don't you come to one of our classes?"

"Oh, I don't think I could right now. I don't have a lot of time. I'm getting married in two months and I have to lose twenty pounds." I blushed. Why did that just pop right out of my mouth? Was it because he was so handsome? Even though I was off the market I still felt the pressing need to embarrass myself in front of handsome men, apparently.

"Oh, are you dieting?" His lips twitched.

"Yes, right now I'm trying out a few different diets."

"Listen to me, you don't need a fad diet or a crazy list of foods that you can and can't eat. If you eat green, you'll reach your natural weight in no time."

"My natural weight?"

"Sure. We're all built a little different, so we all have a weight that is suitable to our body types and genetics. Of course the magazines won't tell you that, but it's the truth."

"Oh?"

"Well, it's my truth." He chuckled. "I like to think I've never been healthier, and it's because I eat everything out of my garden. I won't touch anything that I don't grow."

"What about meat and dairy?"

"I'm a vegan." His smile widened. "I know that's a big change, but even if you do it for just a week or two I guarantee you will see some improvement. Why don't you come to my Monday night class? We garden, but we also talk about healthy sustainable diets. I think you would enjoy it."

I thought about all of the difficulty I'd had with the alarm on my phone and the food I nearly choked on. The twelve-a-day diet did not work for me. I did enjoy the idea of a natural diet—something my body was designed to thrive on.

"Alright, maybe I will. Thanks, Stephen."

"Any time. If you take the path on the right you'll get to the center of the garden. But think about coming to a class, alright?"

"I will." I smiled. Saying that reminded me that Max was still alone with Will.

CHAPTER 17

I continued walking along the path until I could hear voices.

"I'm thinking swans, Max, how do you feel about swans?"

"Actual swans?"

"Oh yes, we couldn't have fake swans."

"But why would we need swans?"

"Swans represent everything that Samantha feels about you."

I could see Max trying to walk away, but Will followed right after him. Max shot me a look with smoldering eyes and tightened lips.

"And just how could you know how Samantha feels about me? You've only just met her."

"Max, it's just his way. He's actually very perceptive." I slipped my arm through his. I could feel the tension in his arm. I looked up into his eyes and noticed the heat there. The meeting obviously wasn't going well.

"Thank you, Samantha. I was just discussing swans

with Max—"

"Oh well, Max is a little afraid of birds."

"I am not afraid of them!"

"Okay, he prefers to avoid them."

"Oh, why didn't you just say so? I will absolutely not get any swans—not a single one," Will said, shaking his head almost violently.

"Good." Max tipped his head toward the fountain in the middle of the garden. "I do think this place is nice though. What do you think, Sammy? Do you enjoy the view?" He lifted an eyebrow just enough to make my heart pound.

"I think it's beautiful." I searched his expression for a hint of what bothered him so much. "Do you really like it?"

His expression softened. "Yes, I really do. I'd be happy to have our wedding here. Is that what you want?"

"Yes." I smiled. "Yes, I think it's perfect—and it's all thanks to Will." I looked over at him. "He's the one who found this place for us."

"It's what I do." Will bowed. He smiled at Max. "Don't worry, Max. By the day of the wedding, we're going to be the best of friends."

Max didn't answer; he only nodded. I could sense that something was quite off about his behavior.

"Are there papers we should sign?" Max looked over at Arielle.

"No need, I'll take care of everything." Will smiled.

"Yes I will."

"I see what you're doing there." Max quirked a brow. "I guess that we'll be going then."

"Thanks again." I smiled at them both before we walked back toward the car. Max opened my door for me, but he didn't speak.

"Max, are you okay?"

"Let's just get going."

I settled into my seat. When Max closed his door I looked over at him. "What's going on? Do you not like the garden?"

"I'm not sure that I'm ready to talk about it." He started the car.

"Max, what is it?" My heart started to pound. "Did I do something wrong?"

Max started driving. "I just need to calm down. Can we just not talk about it right now?"

I stared at him for a long moment. It made my heart ache to think that he was angry and unwilling to share it with me. Of course I knew it had to happen now and then, but it was quite rare with us.

In the awkward silence that filled the car, I thought about everything that had happened that afternoon. I wasn't sure what I'd done to upset him.

The alarm on my phone started beeping to let me know that it was time to eat again. I fumbled with the phone to turn off the alarm. Before I could, Max snatched it out of my hand.

"Max?"

"It's off." He handed it back to me.

"Please tell me what's wrong? Is the alarm bothering you?"

"No, it's not the alarm." Max drew a deep breath and then pulled over to the side of the road. "Alright, the truth?"

"Yes, please."

"I don't understand why you're doing this."

"Doing what?"

"These crazy diets, Sammy. You know how much I love you. You're so beautiful and sexy—and everything I want. Why isn't that enough for you?"

"Max." I reached out and took his hand. "You have no idea how wonderful it makes me feel to know that you see me that way. But you also know how hard I've worked to get to my goal weight. I'm not there, Max. I made some mistakes. I want to be sure that I can lose the weight before the wedding. I just don't understand why that upsets you."

"Why?" He looked over at me. "Stephen is why."

"Stephen?"

"Did you really think I didn't see the way you looked at him? You practically fainted."

CHAPTER 18

My cheeks burned with embarrassment. "Max, that was just a knee-jerk reaction—probably the pineapple still getting out of my system."

"Or maybe it's not our wedding that you are trying to lose weight for. Maybe my opinion about your beauty doesn't matter to you because it's just not as important to you anymore."

"Max! How can you even say that?"

"How can't I, Sammy?" He narrowed his eyes. "What am I supposed to think when my attraction to you isn't enough?"

I sighed and wiped a hand across my mouth. "Max."

"What? Please, enlighten me."

"How a woman looks or wants to look isn't always about pleasing a man. I've had a look—a size—in mind for my wedding day for years. Not because I want to please you, or Stephen, or the minister, but because that is how I see myself. That's how I want to look—it's how I feel inside."

Max gave my hand a light squeeze. "I can understand that. I can. But these diets worry me. You're going from surviving on juice to eating constantly. What's next?"

"Whatever works." I hardened my gaze. "I'm not going to give up on my goal. I want to achieve it, and I'm going to try what I have to until I do achieve it. You say that I'm beautiful and that you love me. Well, this desire is part of me."

"I'm trying to understand, Sammy. If it's important to you, then of course it's important to me. I just wish you would relax and enjoy this. I feel like we barely get to see each other. I don't know." He shook his head. "Maybe I'm just expecting too much."

"No, you're not, Max. I'm sorry." I drew his hand to my lips. "I have been caught up in so much. We haven't had much time together. It's time to get our priorities straight, I guess." I paused and looked into his eyes. "The wedding's still on, though, right?"

"Sammy." He stared hard at me. "I love you, Samantha. I would walk across shattered glass to marry you. But this is what concerns me—that you would even ask me that."

I frowned. I knew that he was right. If I were one of the characters from my book, my insecurity would be a major issue to work on. I'd made great progress on it, but I was blindsided by my weight gain.

"You're right. I love you, Max."

"I love you too." He leaned over to kiss me. The

moment that his lips touched mine I felt the surreal rush of our connection. Max drove me back to my apartment as if he was fine, but I could still see the tension in his expression.

"Cake tasting with Will tomorrow?" I met his eyes.

"I will, I will." He winked at me.

"Alright, good night." I kissed his cheek and then slid out of the car. As I walked up to my apartment the alarm went off again on my phone, prompting me to eat yet again.

I slumped down on the couch. I didn't like to fight with Max, especially when he was right. But I also couldn't give up on the idea that I would be able to fit into that dress. I fell asleep that night with a full stomach and an ache in my heart.

The next day started out with a call from my mother.

"I have my tickets to fly in. I can't wait to get there. I can't wait to see you in your wedding dress. You've slimmed down so much that I just know that you'll look stunning."

I knew that my mother meant well, but I didn't feel like I looked stunning—especially not after seeing the latest numbers on my scale that morning. I was more discouraged than ever.

"Thanks, Mom, but I put on a few pounds."

"Oh, Samantha, this is the worst time to let yourself balloon up."

"I know, Mom." I frowned. "I'm trying to fix it."

"I bet. Don't worry, Samantha, the important thing is that Max loves you. You'll have a beautiful wedding."

I knew my mother didn't meant to upset me, but her words rankled my nerves. "Looking forward to it. I have to go now, Mom."

"Go where? You work from home now."

"I know, but I'm going to a gardening class." I decided at that moment that I really was going to go to the class. I wanted a chance to see the gardens again, and I wanted to confront my attraction to Stephen.

Her laughter echoed in my ear. "You and gardening? Oh boy, I wish I was there to see that."

"Thanks, Mom. I love you." I hung up the phone before she could even say it back. I didn't need anything to make me more irritable than I already was.

I frowned as I dialed the number for Cerulean Gardens.

"Hello, Cerulean Gardens."

"Hi, is there a gardening class today?"

"Not until the weekend."

"Oh." I frowned.

"Stephen is always available for private instruction if you'd like to set up an appointment with him."

I raised an eyebrow. A class was one thing. There would be plenty of other people there to keep me on my best behavior. But one on one?

"Alright, is he available today before one?"

"How is nine-thirty?"

I glanced at the clock to see that it was almost nine. "Alright, that's fine."

"Great, and your name?"

I gave her my information. With every word, I wondered if it was a mistake.

LILLIANNA BLAKE

CHAPTER 19

Once I'd arrived at Cerulean Gardens, I thought about going back home. What was I thinking? Obviously I was attracted to Stephen, so why would I put myself in a position to be alone with him?

I closed my eyes. I hadn't felt much of an attraction for another man since I fell in love with Max. Sure, here and there I might feel something, but not the head-turning desire that overtook me when I saw Stephen for the first time.

I was confident that I would not cheat on Max, but I was curious. What was it about Stephen that I found so attractive?

When I walked up to the entrance, I found Stephen waiting for me.

"Samantha." He smiled. "Glad to see you again."

"Glad you could see me. I mean, glad to see you too. I mean, thanks for teaching me."

Stephen laughed. "Don't worry. Once you get your hands dirty, you're going to relax."

I bit into my bottom lip and tried not to let my mind

wander. He didn't have his sleeveless shirt on any more. Instead, he wore a simple red polo shirt. He wasn't covered in sweat and his dark hair wasn't mussed. The allure of the day before had faded, but there was still something that seemed to draw me to him.

"Walk with me," he said.

I fell into step beside him. As we walked he pointed out all of the different plants that grew in the garden. I listened, but I wasn't really hearing his words. I listened to the inflection of his voice, the tenderness of it, the love he felt for what he was describing.

"This is the area we're going to be working in today." He gestured to a raised bed with vines that crawled up a small fence. "We're going to start by adding some friends."

"Friends? I thought this was a private class."

He winked at me. "It is…just you and me—and the worms."

"Worms?"

I watched him pick up a small container.

"See?" He opened the lid to show me tons of writhing worms.

"Oh wow!" I took a step back.

"You're not afraid of worms, are you?"

"No, I've just never seen that many in one place before."

"The worms really help the garden. So we're going to add a few into this one."

"We?"

"Sure, just grab one. Be careful not to squeeze."

I lifted an eyebrow. "Do I get gloves?"

"They're not going to hurt you. I promise."

"I don't know."

"Samantha, look at me."

I looked into his eyes and immediately regretted it. The sudden connection made me feel as if I'd been swept away into a warm safe place. I didn't like it. Or I did like it. I liked it way too much.

"Okay, I'll pick up the worm." I stuck my hand in the container and pulled out a wiggly worm. It wasn't as bad as I thought. I dropped it into the damp soil. Then I added a few more. I was very aware that Stephen was standing close to me.

"Now get your hands in the dirt and move it around a bit." Stephen dug his fingers down into the dirt as if he was massaging it.

"My hands—down in the dirt—with the worms?" I looked up at him.

"Yes, Samantha. Trust me, it will feel so good on your skin. Just dig in deep and really squish the dirt between your fingers. It's really relaxing."

"But, the worms. The dirt is their home. Should I really be invading it? Isn't that disruptive?" I peered at the dirt. I saw the worms moving around in the dirt. My heart sped up. It wasn't that I didn't like bugs and such, or even that I was afraid of them. It was that they had a place in the dirt, and I had a place—not in the dirt.

"Samantha, trust me. Just try it. This is the best way to appreciate and value the food that you're putting into your mouth."

I watched a big beetle crawl over the curve of a ripe tomato. I gritted my teeth and tried not to squeak. Maybe gardening would help my diet after all. I took a deep breath and then snorted out a gnat that had flown up my nose. My hands flew at my face to swat away the bug.

I sighed. I was ready to give up. Then my stubbornness kicked in. I wasn't going to be held back by dirt. I pushed my fingers into the soil.

I was stunned by how warm the dirt was. It was actually quite relaxing to wiggle my fingers around in it. All of the worries I'd had about bugs fled my mind. I lost myself in the motion of churning the dirt.

"Good job…excellent." Stephen patted my shoulder.

It was a friendly pat, but the moment he touched me I felt a surge of protectiveness. I moved a few steps away from him and continued to churn the dirt. In that moment, I knew that no matter how attracted I felt to Stephen, the very thought of a man other than Max touching me felt very wrong.

So, why did I feel such a strong connection to Stephen?

"I highly recommend a diet rich in fruits and vegetables. In fact, a friend of mine follows one called Eat Green. She eats only green foods that grow in the ground."

"Why green?"

"Something about the dark green vegetables having more of the nutrients that she needs." He shrugged. "It can't hurt to eat healthy, can it?"

My alarm rang to remind me that it was time to eat again.

"Here." He handed me a strawberry that he plucked from the garden.

I didn't hesitate to pop it right into my mouth. It tasted delicious, even with a hint of dirt still on it. I smiled at him. "Thanks."

"You're welcome." He smiled back.

We stared at each other for a long moment. I really looked into his eyes. I saw a beautiful man, with a loving spirit, who had a passion for what he did.

Then it struck me.

When was the last time that I'd looked at Max like that? How long had it been since I gazed into his eyes and really recognized who he was inside? I was attracted to Stephen, not because of his muscles or his lovely hair, but because he was passionate and nurturing. Max was both of those things too, but ever since I'd discovered my weight gain I'd cut myself off from him.

"I'm sorry, Stephen, I have to go."

"It's okay." He smiled. "If you ever want to learn more, you know where I am."

"Thanks!"

I turned and ran out of the garden.

CHAPTER 20

I drove straight to Max's house. I didn't want to let another moment pass without re-igniting what I'd shut down between us. I couldn't believe that I'd let my own insecurity separate us yet again. Max accepted and adored me, but that was hard for me to believe—no matter how many time he proved it to me.

As I walked up to his front door a strange sensation caused my heart to pound. This wasn't going to be Max's house much longer. It was going to be our house. I wondered how I'd react to that. It was a cute place with plenty of room. But it wasn't mine. Not yet.

I reached up to knock on the door, then decided to try something different. When Max came to my apartment he'd always had a key and been welcome to let himself in. He told me the same applied to his house, but I'd always knocked.

This time, I decided to use my key. I unlocked the door and walked right in. The house was quiet. It was too late for him to still be sleeping.

"Max?" I roamed through the house.

Our date for the cake tasting was in an hour. Maybe he'd gone for a walk. I decided to sit on his bed and wait for him.

When I walked into the bedroom, I nearly tripped over a pile of dirty clothes on the floor. I grabbed what I could to catch myself—unfortunately it was a less than sturdy lamp, which did nothing to hold me up. I managed to catch the edge of the bed with my other hand, but the lamp went crashing to the floor.

The bathroom door was flung open and Max jumped out with a loud shout. He wore absolutely nothing but a few droplets of water.

"Max!" I looked up at him—I was half on the floor and half on his bed.

"Sammy?" He blinked. He looked from his knocked-over lamp, to me, then down at his own naked body. "I thought you were a burglar!"

He ducked back into the bathroom and grabbed a towel.

When he emerged again I was a little disappointed to see that he was covered up.

"I'm sorry, I thought you weren't here."

Max furrowed a brow. "If you thought I wasn't here then why are you in my bedroom?"

"I was going to wait for you to come back."

"Oh?" He offered a half-smile.

"But then I tripped over your clothes and the lamp."

"Sorry about that. I'll try to be more tidy." He held out his hand to me and helped me to sit down on the edge of the bed. He sat down beside me. The heat from his shower still emanated from his skin. I took a breath of the scent of his soap.

"Max, I'm the one that should be sorry."

"What do you mean? You're always welcome here. Soon this will be your home too." He smiled.

"No, it's not that. I realized that you're right—it isn't even just that we haven't seen that much of one another. It's that when we do, I'm holding back."

Max's eyes narrowed. "What are you trying to say, Sammy?"

"I guess I got caught up in the wedding plans, my books and, well—everything. I feel like I'm disconnected from us."

Max shifted on the bed so that he could look straight at me. "Sammy, you're not having doubts, are you? I'd rather you be honest with me."

"No!" I nearly shouted. "No, I'm not having doubts, Max. At least not about us."

"Then what? Marriage? Is it too fast?"

"No. It's me." I sighed. "I've slipped back into some old patterns."

"That's normal, Sammy." He rubbed my shoulder. "We're going through a huge change in our lives. It's a little scary. Then we start freaking out. I'm sorry about the way I talked to you about Stephen. I trust you, and it's normal to be attracted to other people. I'm not going to say that I like it, but I shouldn't have been so jealous about it."

"I think you were right to be, Max."

"What?" He frowned. "Do you have feelings for him?"

"No. But I saw something in him that I wasn't allowing in us. I shut down our connection—our intimacy."

"I have been feeling a little on the outside lately."

"I'm sorry." I leaned close to him.

He wrapped his arm around my shoulders. "I just want you to be able to trust me. We're going to spend the rest of our lives together. More than anything, I want you to know how much I love you—not only to hear me say it, but to really know it."

"I'm trying." I kissed his cheek.

He kissed the top of my head. "Let's go eat some cake, hm? Or do you have to wait for you alarm?"

"No more alarms." I laughed.

"Good." He sighed with relief.

"Can we just sit here for a little while? Together?"

"Absolutely." He wrapped his other arm around me and pulled me against his chest.

I closed my eyes and breathed to the rhythm of his heartbeat.

CHAPTER 21

When we left for the cake tasting, I asked Max to stop at a local farmer's market.

"I'm going to try eating green." I smiled at him.

"Another crazy diet?" He cringed.

"This is more about eating healthy and providing nutrients to my body."

"Well, I guess that sounds better than pineapple and alarms."

"It'll be great."

I looked around for every green vegetable I could find. The more I smelled the fruits and vegetables, the more certain I was that this diet was going to be right for me.

Once I was loaded up with healthy greens, the idea of tasting cakes was even more appealing.

"So what kind are you thinking? Chocolate? Custard?" I looked over at Max as he drove to the bakery.

"Well, maybe we should wait and see what Will likes." He grinned.

"Oh, let me guess—it will be white chocolate raspberry truffle." I laughed.

"Hey, that sounds pretty good." Max grinned.

When we pulled into the parking lot of the bakery, I could see Will by the front door. He waved to us with such enthusiasm that he nearly dropped his binder.

"He sure puts in the effort." Max chuckled.

"Be nice. I like Will."

"I like him too. I think." Max grinned.

"I brought forks!" Will waved tiny silver forks in the air. "We have to get a final decision today, kids, or the baker is not going to be able to have the cake ready in time."

His words reminded me of how little time there was left before the wedding. We were already putting the final touches on it. That meant I only had about a week before I went back for the next fitting of my dress.

I looked down at the pudge of my belly and frowned. Was it really a good idea to be eating cake right now?

"Ready?" Max slid his arm around my waist.

"Yup." I managed a smile.

As we walked into the bakery I noticed a sign in the window. "Oh, that looks interesting." I started to point it out to Max, but Will already had his attention. I skimmed over the sign to keep my eyes off the assortment of cakes. It was dotted with pictures of people trying to overcome obstacles. I was confused at first until I read that it was a race. "How fun." I laughed as I remembered the obstacle courses my friends and I would set up when we were kids. It made sense that some people would still like it as adults.

"Sammy, do you want to try the white chocolate? Will recommends it." Max winked at me.

I held back my laughter.

We sat down at the table with the cakes spread out before us. Each one looked more delicious than the last. My stomach rumbled with desire.

"Here you go." Will handed me one of the silver forks. "Give it a try." He pushed one of the plates toward me.

I sank the fork into the cake. I tried not to think about the way my belly strained against the waistband of my jeans. The bite of cake melted in my mouth.

"Oh, it's so good." I sighed with pleasure.

"Mm, so is this one." Max fed me a bite of the cake that he'd tried.

We went back and forth for some time feeding each other cake. I was about to feed him another bite when all of the sugar hit my system. I started to get dizzy. I missed his mouth with the cake and smashed it into his cheek instead.

"Oops, no cake smashing until the wedding!" Will laughed.

"Sorry, Max."

He swept the cake off his cheek and stuck his finger in his mouth. "Mm, still good. My turn." He picked up a piece of cake and smashed it right into my face. I was so shocked that I didn't even wipe it off.

"Max, why did you do that?"

"I thought we were having fun." He frowned. "Food fight?"

"Not in my bakery!" An older man with sharp blue eyes glared at Max from behind the counter. "Clean that mess up, young man, or I won't be baking any cakes for you."

Will cringed. "I guess I should have warned you. Alonzo can be a little picky about who he bakes for."

"Max!" I reached for a napkin in the same moment that Max did. Our hands bumped together and we knocked a plate of cake onto the floor.

"Out!" Alonzo shouted. "How dare you waste my delicious cake? Out with you both!"

"Alonzo, please. It was an accident! I will make it up to you. I will!" Will pleaded with him.

"Out, I said!" Alonzo pointed to the door.

"I think we better listen." Max handed me the napkin.

I couldn't even speak, I was so angry.

CHAPTER 22

I wiped the cake off my face as we walked out of the bakery.

Max laughed and kissed my cheek. "Mm, tasty."

"Max, it's not funny!" I threw my napkin at him.

"Sure it is." Max laughed again. "You should see your face right now."

"I don't want to see it! I wanted to pick out a cake for our wedding! You couldn't be mature long enough for us to do that!" The words flew out of my mouth. I didn't mean them—at least I didn't think I did—but they just kept coming out.

"Can you lower your voice, Sammy?" Max narrowed his eyes. My shouts had drawn a few onlookers.

"I won't! I'm working so hard to make this wedding happen, and you're acting like it's just a game!"

"I am not!"

"No? What about the honeymoon, Max? Have you even planned it yet?"

"It's a surprise."

"Oh yeah, I bet. Surprise, we're going to Motel 6 because I forgot to make reservations! Ha ha!"

"Sammy! Is that what you really think—that I'm some kind of irresponsible jerk?"

"Well, did we pick out a cake?"

"You started it!"

"I got dizzy!"

"Probably because of those crazy diets that you've been on! I told you that was a bad idea!"

"Max, take me home right now!"

"Gladly." He marched over to the car and jerked open my door for me. Will stared, like a deer in headlights, as I stomped after him.

"Uh, guys, we still need to talk about the cake!"

We both slammed the car doors shut at the same time. Max started the car and backed out of the parking lot.

Neither of us spoke as he drove toward my apartment. Every little sound he made bugged me. I wanted to reach out and pinch his nose shut to stop him from breathing. I wanted to flick him in the cheek to get him to stop clenching his teeth. He had no right to be mad. He was the one that had ruined the cake tasting.

"Here." He parked in front of my apartment. He didn't move to get out of the car or look at me.

"Max, we should talk about this."

"I don't want to talk about it, Sammy. I think you made it very clear what your opinion is of me. Here I thought you knew me better than anyone else, but it turns out, you don't know me at all." He reached across me and popped open my door. "Bye, Sammy."

I took a sharp breath in. Max had never been so rude to me. My heart started to race.

"Max, we should really talk this out."

"Not now. I need to be alone."

"Max—"

"Sammy, I don't want to hear anything more about how you need to lose weight, or these wild diets, or how there isn't enough time left before the wedding. Please. I just need some time away from all of this craziness."

I stared at him with disbelief. Did he just call me crazy?

My nostrils flared. My hands balled into fists. I got out of the car before I said anything I'd regret. I stormed into my apartment and slammed the door shut. Then I turned around to face it.

I was sure that Max would follow after me. He would be there any second to apologize for the way he'd talked to me. I just knew it.

After five minutes I walked over to the window to check the parking lot. His car was gone. The realization of what had happened hit me so hard that I landed on the couch, feeling as if all my breath had just left my body. My face grew hot.

"What just happened?" I stared at my hands. They were shaking and still smeared with frosting. "Is the wedding off?"

I grabbed my phone and called Stephanie. Through my sobs, I told her what had happened.

"Wait, you started a food fight with Max? And he got mad?"

"No! It was a misunderstanding. And I got mad! I mean, I really lost it—and then so did he."

"Samantha, it's okay. I'm sure once he cools off he'll call to apologize."

"No, I don't think he will." I sniffed. "He was so upset. He said I didn't know him at all! Why would he want to marry someone who doesn't know him at all?"

"He was just upset—just like you were. Fights are going to happen now and then."

"But why are we fighting so much before the wedding? I don't like this. What if he's finally had it with me? What if he decides to cancel the wedding?" I moaned into the phone.

"I know why you're upset, but you have to get control of yourself. Ever since you started dieting, your moods have been a little wild."

"So it's my fault!"

"No, that's not what I'm saying, Sammy. It's just that I've seen a big change in you ever since the dress fitting. Maybe this is a sign that you need to get back in touch with yourself a little more."

I sighed. "Maybe. I have been a bit of a loose cannon."

"Alright, so why not do something that helps you to calm down?"

"You're right. I should take a meditation class. I'll see when there's one I can go to."

"Good. Everything will be fine. You'll see."

After I hung up with Stephanie my tears stopped falling so fast. I wiped at my eyes. I'd planned to make Max a delicious vegetarian meal, but I guessed he wasn't interested in that now. I decided to prepare it anyway for myself.

While my assortment of vegetables steamed on the stove, I checked my computer for the next available meditation class. It wasn't until the next afternoon. I signed up for it, then decided to check my blog.

I updated my readers with the information about the new diet I was trying. Then I wrote about how diet can affect your moods. As I posted the update, I smelled something strange. All of a sudden I remembered the vegetables on the stove.

"Oh no!" I jumped up and ran for the stove. The vegetables that I intended to steam to a perfect crisp were a pile of mush. I turned down the heat and tried to grab the pan off the stove.

"Ouch!" The handle was hot. As I dropped the pan back down on the stove there was a knock on the door.

LILLIANNA BLAKE

CHAPTER 23

I rinsed my hand in the sink to cool it off and then ran for the door. I jerked it open.

"Sammy." Max leaned against the side of the door.

"Max." I frowned. My hand still throbbed.

"I'm sorry."

"So am I."

"Can I come in?"

I nodded and stepped back from the door. He looked at my red palm. "What happened?"

"Oh, I grabbed the handle of the pan without a potholder. I'm okay."

He frowned and took a closer look. "I can't believe the way I talked to you. I'm really sorry, Sammy."

"I'm sorry too, Max. I overreacted about the cake. You were just trying to have fun."

"I should have realized that you didn't mean to get the cake on me. I just thought, maybe fun Sammy was back." He cringed. "I didn't mean it like that."

"No, you're right." I sighed. "I haven't been much fun lately. I'm sorry."

"No, you're right. I haven't been pulling my weight with the wedding."

"Max, I just want us to be happy." I looked into his eyes. "Are we okay?"

He smiled. "We're always going to be okay. I'm sorry if I made you feel any different."

"I promise I'll try to be more fun."

"You are fun." He kissed my forehead. "I just want you to be happy. That's all I want."

"I am." I smiled at him.

"Good. I'm going to go, okay."

I started to offer him dinner, then I remembered the mush I'd made. "Okay. I love you, Max."

"I love you too." He kissed me.

After he left I sat down with my vegetable mush. My mind still flitted from possibility to possibility. Were Max and I really okay?

I feasted on vegetables all day the next day. I wanted to make sure that I ate as many healthy greens as I could. I hoped that the good nutrition would balance out what the less healthy diets had done to me.

By the time I left for the meditation class I'd eaten half of the groceries I bought.

As I stepped into the meditation space I was flooded with a sense of peace. It had been so long since I meditated. I realized that was a big part of what was missing from my life.

Not long after I'd arrived, six other people filed in. One in particular drew my attention. I thought she was stunning. Her tall and slender figure made her look sculpted. Her movements were graceful and smooth. Her plain features had a peaceful glow. I watched as she walked to the center of the room and sat down.

The entire time that the teacher led us through the guided meditation, I was distracted by the presence of the woman. I felt drawn to her—similar to what I'd felt with Stephen.

At some point my mind drifted enough that I could relax. The wildness of my emotions became very clear. I'd let everything get out of control. All of my beliefs about myself had become colored with doubts—all because my dress hadn't fit. I did my best to release the thoughts and emotions.

When I surfaced from my meditation, my stomach cramped. My eyes widened. All of the vegetables I'd eaten seemed to be having a less than ideal impact on my digestive system. I gulped as I wondered if it was going to be a repeat of my recent yoga class.

I opened my eyes to see the woman in the center of the room. She was so perfect and peaceful. I hoped I wouldn't let one rip and ruin the moment. She spoke to the teacher for a few minutes and then walked toward the door.

I stood up carefully. I didn't want to risk any

spontaneous explosions. Once I was on my feet I made my way toward her. I was quite curious about her.

I caught up with her at the door of the room. "Excuse me, can I ask you a question?"

"Sure." She smiled at me.

"I don't mean to sound rude or crazy, but I'm trying to lose weight for my wedding and I noticed how thin you are. Is there a special diet that you follow?" I bit my lip and hoped that she wouldn't be offended.

"Oh, I'm a breathatarian."

"A what?"

"I breathe to satiate my hunger—and to keep my body in a spiritual state."

"You don't eat anything at all?" I frowned. I hated to think of this beautiful woman stuck in the throes of an eating disorder.

"Oh no, I do eat. I saw a health consultant who told me the minimum amount of calories I need to eat each day to remain healthy. I eat that, and if I get hungry at other times, I just breathe through the hunger until it's gone. You see, our body yearns for more than just food. Many times it just needs a little oxygen boost."

"Wow, that's really interesting."

"Might be something to try. But it's really a lifestyle, not a diet."

"Do you think you could show me a few techniques?"

She looked at me for a long moment. "I don't know."

"I'm sorry, I didn't mean to be rude."

"No, it's not that. I just don't want you to overdo it. It's something you have to be careful about when you're just starting out."

"I will be. I promise."

"Alright, I'll teach you a few things. But if you start to feel dizzy or lightheaded, then you have to stop, okay?"

"Okay."

She demonstrated the long deep breath that was used to sustain the body. It amazed me that she could involve so many of her muscles in breathing. As she exhaled all of the muscles relaxed.

"You pair it with a visualization of your mind and body being nourished. It's important to remember that this is about spiritual nourishment, not starving yourself."

"I'll remember. Thank you so much for taking the time to show me."

"No problem. Good luck." She waved to me as she left the class.

LILLIANNA BLAKE

CHAPTER 24

As I walked out the door I tried to take the deep breath that the woman had shown me. It wasn't until my belly started to stretch that I remembered my little vegetable problem. I released the air in a burst through my nose and waddled across the parking lot to my car—okay, waddling may be a strong word to describe it, but it's sure how I felt.

I'd just made it to the door, when all of the gas escaped me in one long loud explosion. I even burped at the same time. I looked around to see if anyone had heard. The perfect woman was already gone.

I sighed with relief and opened the door to my car.

"Uh, Sammy?"

I spun around fast and found Max behind me. He stood a few feet away—and then took one more step back.

"Sorry to startle you. Stephanie said that you'd be here." He cleared his throat.

My heart pounded. Had he heard the epic flatulence?

"Are you feeling okay?"

"Peaceful. Very peaceful." My eyes spread wide.

"Oh?"

I could tell he was trying not to smile.

"You heard it, didn't you?"

"Maybe."

"Oh my god."

"Don't worry about it, Sammy—it's just a bodily function."

"Now I'm fat and flatulent; just great."

"Sammy, you're not fat." He rolled his eyes. "I thought you were over that?"

"Why are you here?"

"I wanted to take you to dinner."

I thought about how gassy I still felt and my desire to experiment with breathing instead of eating.

"I don't think I'm up for it tonight, Max."

"Okay." He shrugged and shoved his hands into his pockets. "I guess I'll be going then."

"Max—"

"It's fine. You have your fitting for the dress at the end of the week, right?"

"Yes." I cringed. I couldn't believe it was already time.

"Do you want me to go with you?"

"You know it's bad luck to see me in the dress before the wedding."

"I don't believe in any of that. If you need my support, I'll be there."

"I'll be fine. Stephanie is going with me."

"Okay, good." He leaned in and gave me a quick kiss. "Night. You might wanna roll your car windows down."

"Max!"

He walked away laughing.

Over the next few days I did my best to breathe instead of eat. I stuck to my green food for my base calories and then breathed like crazy when I craved more food. At first it was very difficult, but as the hours passed, it became easier. I enjoyed focusing on my breath and refreshing my mind with beautiful visualizations.

I did feel a little dizzy pretty much all of the time, though—hint: do not try this yourself!

The morning of the dress fitting, I woke up with a sense of dread. The day had come. I felt sick to my stomach as I waited for Stephanie to pick me up. I didn't even want to think about putting the dress on. I could tell from my belly—and from the numbers on the scale—that I wasn't going to fit into it. It broke my heart to think that I'd have to let it out. I wondered if I'd need to have it let out even more—was it possibly that I'd actually gained weight since my last fitting?

When Stephanie knocked on the door I opened it with a frown and drooped shoulders.

"What's wrong?"

"I don't think the dress is going to fit."

"So, she'll let it out. No big deal." Stephanie smiled.

I knew that she was trying to make me feel better. But it wasn't going to work.

"You know what you need? The perfect outfit to wear." She walked past me to my bedroom.

I sighed as she began searching through my closet.

"What I wear today isn't going to matter, Stephanie."

"Trust me." She spent a few more minutes searching around, then she pulled out a sundress. "This is it."

"Alright." I shook my head and took the dress.

"Go change." She shooed me toward the bathroom.

When I came back out she still had her head in my closet.

"What are you doing?"

"Oh, sorry, it's just you have some great pieces in here. I'll have to borrow something some time."

I smiled at her words. That did make me feel a little better. "Let's go get this over with."

When we arrived at the boutique, Gail greeted us at the door. "Hello, beautiful ladies." She smiled.

"Hi, Gail." I couldn't quite look at her. "I guess we better try the dress on again."

"Listen, Samantha, I might have made a mistake, but I can fix it if I did."

She seemed very nervous, which in turn made my heart pound with dread even more than it already was.

"What is it, Gail?"

"Well, I got a little confused and thought you wanted

me to go ahead and let the dress out. So I did. Then I realized that we were supposed to have one more fitting before I did that. I'm so sorry."

I frowned. "It's okay. I wasn't going to fit into it anyway."

Stephanie gave me a half-hug. "Let's see it on you!"

I tried to muster up some enthusiasm.

LILLIANNA BLAKE

CHAPTER 25

As I changed into the dress, it did feel much more comfortable. I walked out of the dressing room.

Stephanie clapped her hands. "You look gorgeous!"

"I do?" I stepped in front of the mirror. I couldn't even bring myself to smile.

"What's wrong, Samantha?" Gail stepped up beside me.

"It just looks different." I stared at the dress in the mirror.

"I only let it out a little." Gail frowned. "Nothing else has changed about the dress."

I looked over at Stephanie and shook my head. "I think I just need to get a different dress."

"Are you kidding?" Stephanie's eyes widened. "You're in love with this dress."

"I guess it just doesn't look the way I expected it to. I just don't think—with my weight—it works."

"It's very close to the wedding to consider a change like that." Gail shook her head. "Samantha, it's almost the exact same size that it was."

"But it's not right." I turned away from the mirror. "This is horrible. Everything is going wrong."

"What's going wrong?" Stephanie frowned. "You and Max are happy. You found a beautiful place for the wedding. You have a great wedding planner."

"But we've been fighting and distant with one another, and the wedding was supposed to be at the chapel, and I was the one who was supposed to plan the wedding, and my dress was supposed to fit!" Tears sprang to my eyes and I tried to catch my breath. I couldn't stop the panic that seized me.

Stephanie stood up and wrapped her arms around me.

"Samantha, you're just having wedding jitters, that's all. What have you eaten today?"

I frowned. I didn't want to answer. In a last-ditch effort to lose a few more pounds, I hadn't eaten anything at all.

"I'm taking you to get something to eat. Get out of that dress. We're going shopping for the bridal shower, and we're going to have a delicious lunch. Don't make any decisions about the dress just yet. Alright?"

"Alright." I nodded.

As Gail helped me out of the dress she spoke to me in a quiet tone.

"I hope I'm not overstepping here, Samantha, but may I share something with you?"

"Yes, of course."

"I've been married for fifty years now."

"Fifty years?" I smiled. "That's amazing."

"It is. But it was also hard, hon. It was rough to stay together that long."

"Why, aren't you in love?"

"Sure we are—we always have been. But life doesn't care if you're in love Samantha. Life gets difficult. It makes you do and say things you never thought you would. Sometimes it can even turn you against the person you love most in the world. My husband and I have stayed together this long, because whenever something got hard, we faced it together. We found a way to deal with those things and didn't let them tear us apart. Your wedding is just the beginning of your life together. There will be hard times—that's something you can count on. The important thing is the love you have for one another. It's the only thing that will get you through."

I frowned as her words sunk in. "You're right."

"I'll leave you to change."

As she walked away tears welled up in my eyes. If I couldn't handle getting married how was I going to handle marriage?

As Stephanie and I shopped for the bridal shower, I tried to be positive. My thoughts matter, I reminded myself. But it was hard for me to be upbeat. I wanted my wedding to be a certain way, and it never seemed more impossible.

"I was thinking of these types of favors at the dinner." Stephanie held up tiny umbrellas for me to see.

I nodded a little. "Sure, they look good."

"Or maybe these?" She picked up another set.

"Whatever you think is best."

"Samantha? Earth to Samantha?" She laughed and waved her hand in front of my face.

"I'm so sorry, I'm just a little distracted."

"What's going on? Planning your bridal shower is supposed to be fun!"

I took a deep breath. I willed it to fill and sustain me as it had done in the past few days. "I'm not losing any weight. Why can't I just drop a few more pounds?"

"Oh, Samantha." Stephanie frowned. "You're too worried about that. The dress fits you perfectly now. Why worry about your weight when the dress is already let out?"

"Stephanie, that would be admitting failure. I simply can't admit failure."

"Sometimes we fail at things. It's not an ending, it's an opportunity to think from a new perspective, or move in a new direction. Think of all the times that you thought your relationships were failures."

"This is not cheering me up." I sighed.

"No, really, think about it. You were devastated each time. You thought it was an ending. But each of those relationship led you down the path toward Max, and in the end, you're in the most amazing relationship. You're about to marry the man of your dreams—someone you've had a crush on for many years. How can that be a failure?"

I thought about it for a moment. "I guess I never looked at it that way."

"Of course you didn't. That's because people get blinded by their failure. They see it as an ending, rather than a beginning."

"A beginning." I nodded a little. "That's a good point."

"So maybe you won't be the exact weight that you wanted to be for your wedding, but will that change anything else about the day?"

"In theory, no—but I don't know, I can't explain it. I worked so hard to lose weight. I don't want to end up looking huge in my wedding pictures."

"Alright." Stephanie hugged me. "I get it. But you can't let it take over your mind. What diet are you on right now?"

"Breathing."

"What?"

"I eat a small amount of calories and then take breaths whenever I get hungry. It's supposed to stop the hunger."

"Are you kidding me?" Stephanie stared at me. "This has gone too far, Samantha. Juicing is one thing, but now you're pretty much starving yourself."

"I'm not. I—"

"—Would you tell any of your readers to do something like that?" Stephanie interrupted me, shaking her head. "What would you say to me if I was doing that diet?"

My defenses fell.

CHAPTER 26

I looked at my friend and realized that if Stephanie had told me the same thing about a diet she was on, I'd lose my mind and buy her a cheeseburger.

"Samantha, maybe you're not losing weight *because* of these crazy diets. Why not just forget about it for a little while? Give your mind and body a few days to rest?"

"But there is so little time left." I blinked back tears.

"And you should be excited by how close the wedding is." Stephanie squeezed my shoulder. "These should be the best moments of your life, not the hardest."

I took another deep breath. I knew she was right. My stomach was empty. It was gnawing on itself. My emotions were out of whack. It was all because of me and what I'd been putting myself through—all for the sake of losing a few pounds.

"Okay." I nodded. "You're right. I'm going to take a break from the crazy diets and everything else. And I do like the umbrellas." I grinned at my friend, thankful for her honesty and support.

"Great." Stephanie smiled.

As we picked out the rest of the decorations, I did start to feel excited. I looked forward to getting together with friends I hadn't seen in a while. I looked forward to just being able to enjoy the party without counting calories or breaths.

I thought of Max and how frustrated he'd become with my dieting. He was worried about me. At a time when we should be celebrating our upcoming marriage, he was worried instead.

I knew that it was time to turn everything around.

Every time I tried to reconnect with Max we ended up butting heads. There was just too much tension. We weren't even married yet, and we were already struggling.

I thought about the advice that Gail had given me about marriage. She'd told me that there would be obstacles, that it was not about having a smooth ride, but about being able to overcome those obstacles together as a team.

It reminded me of the flyer I'd seen in the bakery window—about the couples race that was coming up in our area. Max liked to be active, but he wasn't much for exercising just for the sake of exercising. He enjoyed playing sports, but my coordination did not make catching and throwing easy. Maybe the race would be perfect for us.

I stopped by his house. This time I knocked.

When he opened the door he was frowning. "Now we're back to knocking?"

"Oh no, I just didn't want to startle you."

"I told you that this is your house now too. You shouldn't knock."

I could already see where we were headed—right toward an accidental argument. "Max, I don't want to fight."

"I'm not fighting. Just because I'm talking—"

"Max!" I kissed him hard—so hard that he tripped over the threshold. We stumbled into the house together and ended up tangled up on the floor of the front hallway. I started to pull away to apologize but Max pulled me close. We kissed for a few minutes, sprawled on the floor, with the door wide open.

There it was—the connection. I smiled through the kiss as it blossomed between us.

Seeming to be a bit out of breath, he pulled away and looked into my eyes.

"I'm sorry. I guess I was fighting."

"I don't want to fight any more." I returned his gaze. "It's time that we started acting like a team again."

"I agree." He helped me to my feet and closed the door. "So how do we do that?"

"How do you feel about obstacle courses?"

"Huh?"

"Well, I realize we haven't done anything fun together

in a long time. We go out to dinner and watch movies, but we haven't really played together."

"Okay. You're right." He nodded.

"There's this local race."

"I don't want to do any marathons." He shook his head.

"It's not a marathon. It's a short race. It's an obstacle course, and we have to run through it as a team. Like there's walls to climb—we have to boost each other up over them—mazes to figure out and some other stuff. I don't know all of the details just yet. I thought it would be a fun way for us to blow off some steam and get our minds focused on one another again."

"If you want to do it, I'm willing to try. It sounds like it could be fun."

"Great, because we have to start training today!"

"Training?" He laughed.

"I'm serious."

"What does training mean?"

"It means we have to spend time together." I grinned.

"Well, then, I'm all in." He kissed me again.

The race was four days before the wedding.

We spent the next week and a half training every chance we got. Our training sessions usually turned into make-out sessions, but the important thing was that we were together and connected.

By the day before the race, I could barely contain my excitement. I sat across from Will on my couch and listened as he ran through the final checklist of items for the wedding.

"Okay, so now we have everything lined up. I will make sure it's perfect, I will."

"It can't not be perfect." I smiled.

"Don't worry, I'll make sure it is."

"No, I mean, no matter what happens it will be perfect, because I'm marrying Max."

"Aw, how sweet. It's good to hear that. What are you two doing tomorrow? Maybe we could have brunch together at the gardens."

"No, we're running a race."

"What?" Will's eyes widened.

"It's a special race. It's an obstacle course—with all kinds of tests, and mud and—"

"—and absolutely not!" Will stood up and glared down at me.

I hadn't seen his angry face before.

"What do you mean?"

"Those races can cause injuries! That's why you have to sign a release! How are you going to look hobbling down the aisle in a cast?"

My eyes widened at the idea. "I don't think that's going to happen."

"But it could, Samantha! It could!"

"Will, we're doing the race."

"You will not, you will not!"

I stood up from the couch and put my hands on my hips. "Oh yes we will!"

He sighed and took a step back. "Fine. I guess if it's that important to you, I have no choice. But mark my words that it's not my fault if you end up with a black eye instead of the bride's glow that we're going for."

"Will, you worry too much. It's going to be great!"

"Ridiculous!" He huffed. "I can't even imagine what would make you think this was a good idea."

"Max and I have had a great time practicing for it. Together we're unstoppable."

Will nodded with a light smile. "I get it. But I still don't like it."

CHAPTER 27

Even after Will's warning I was excited about the race.

The bridal shower would be next and then the big day! I couldn't believe it was almost time to be married to the love of my life.

Even though I'd started eating an average diet again, I found myself losing weight as a result of the training that Max and I had been doing together. It wasn't as much as I'd originally wanted to lose, but I was proud of each and every pound.

Once I'd relaxed a bit about it and actually shared an enjoyable activity with Max, the weight had begun to come off once again. I hoped that I'd continue to lose some weight after the wedding, but I still had no idea what the honeymoon would entail. Max wouldn't even give me a hint.

It wasn't easy not to know something so important, but it was important to Max to surprise me.

I spent the rest of my day resting and stretching. I

knew that the next day would be a killer, but I still looked forward to it. It would be one more task that Max and I could check off of the bucket list we were destined to create together.

The next morning Max and I met at the location of the race.

"Are you ready for this?" I grinned at him.

"Are you kidding?" He leaned over to kiss me. "I can't wait."

"Go!"

Max and I tore off toward the first obstacle, as did the other ten couples that were participating. It was a wall of rocks all piled up on top of each other. I thought it would be very easy to get over at first—just a little climbing— but when I put my foot on the first rock, it slid right out from under me. The rocks were loose, which meant that every time I stepped on one the pile shifted.

"Max, how are we going to do this?" I didn't want to give up on the first obstacle. Several of the other couples were having the same problem.

"Let me see if I can get to the top." Max took off up the rocks.

I frowned. "Max, we're supposed to do it together!"

Max got about halfway up and then lost his footing and slid right back down. "It's impossible." He shook his head.

"It can't be impossible. We just have to figure it out."

"Alright." Max nodded. "Let's see. Maybe if we hold on to one another we can distribute our weight enough to create a stable path up the rocks."

"Good idea." I grabbed his hands. We started to climb, but our bodies wobbled in different directions. I tipped forward and nearly knocked us both over. We got our balance, but the rocks slid out from under us again.

"Nope, it's not working." He sighed.

"Maybe if we hold on to each other by the elbows." I showed him what I meant. "It'll help us stay more stable."

"Okay." He smiled. "I'd do anything to hold onto you." He winked.

"Max! Stop being sexy and distracting."

"Stop being sexy? I don't think that's possible, do you?"

"Max! We're never going to make it to the top if you keep talking to me like that."

"Hm? But we already did!" He grinned. "Look!"

I looked and gasped at how high we were. I grabbed him tight around the waist.

"Now who's distracting who?" He laughed.

Once we were down the other side of the rocks, there was a big pool of mud to wade through. I tried to remember how good the dirt had felt on my hands. We sloshed through the mud. It wasn't hard at first until I slipped. Max caught me. Then he slipped. I pulled him up out of the mud and we made our way across the pit. By the time we reached the edge we were both covered in mud.

"Wow, that was wild." I looked ahead to the next obstacle. It was a tunnel that we had to crawl through. It was too narrow for us to fit side-by-side. "Who's going in first?"

"I'll go." Max started to crawl in.

I crawled in behind him. It was very dark inside the tunnel. We moved a few feet, then were hit by icy water. It sprayed right at us as we crawled. Max bore the brunt of it because he was in the front.

"Are you okay?"

"I'm okay." Max sputtered. "I don't know if I can make it all the way, though. Sammy, this is crazy."

"You can do it! I'm right behind you—just keep moving forward." I encouraged him throughout the tunnel until we finally neared the end. I saw light and then Max disappeared with a scream.

"Max?" I lunged after him, only to find that there was nothing under me. The tunnel opened to a huge water slide. I landed in the shallow pool at the bottom.

Max swam over to me. "Are you alright?"

"I'm great." I laughed. "Let's do it again!"

"It's not over yet." Max pointed to the last section of the race.

It was a mixture of crawling under and crawling over obstacles, each with their own deterrent. The first one was covered in thick sandpaper. The second was coated in something foul and sticky, and the third spun so fast that it was a blur.

I tried crawling onto the sandpaper, but it tore at my skin.

"I don't think I can get across this."

"Ouch." Max peered at the scratch on my skin. "Here." He pulled off his shirt and spread it across the sandpaper.

"Thanks!" I smiled at him and crawled across using his shirt to protect me. When I got over to the other side, the shirt was in shreds. "How are you going to get across?"

Max gritted his teeth. "I'll get across." He started to climb on.

"No! Wait!" I hesitated a moment. Then I pulled off my shirt and spread it over the obstacle for him. Luckily, I was wearing a sports bra, but I still felt pretty naked.

"Thanks, Sammy, but now you're really distracting." He winked at me and crawled over.

My shirt became tattered by the rough surface as well.

We crawled through the sticky mess together.

"Ugh." The smell was enough to make me want to vomit.

"We got this. We're almost done!"

"I'm going, I'm going." I laughed in Max's direction.

The last obstacle spun so fast it seemed impossible to get over.

"We're going to have to do it together—at the same time." He grabbed my hand.

We scrambled up on top of the spinning tube, only to get thrown off. Over and over we hit the ground.

"I don't know if we're going to make it." I frowned.

"Hey, we got this far." Max was out of breath and covered in sweat. "We can't give up now."

I thought about what Will had said about hobbling down the aisle. As sore as my body was, I could see hobbling as a real possibility.

"Alright, one more time."

We grabbed onto each other and held on tight as we fought the spin of the tube. When we hit the ground again I groaned, but Max cheered. "We did it!"

"What?" I opened my eyes. We were on the other side of the obstacle. "We did it!" I grabbed his hands and jumped up and down with him. We didn't even mind that other couples rushed past us to the finish line.

We may not have won the race, but we won something much better.

Max and I were a team again.

CHAPTER 28

It took two full days for me to recover from the race. My body was still a little sore when it was time for the bridal shower.

I pulled on the dress I'd chosen for the party and heard the door of my apartment open.

"Babe?"

"I'm in here."

"Are you excited?"

"Very." I laughed, walking out to greet Max.

He wore a t-shirt and jeans. It didn't matter what he wore, he was always gorgeous to me.

"Wow, you look amazing." He took my hand and spun me around in a circle. "Are you sure I can't go with you?"

"Not this time." I grinned.

"Alright, fine." He stuck his bottom lip out. I kissed it.

"Don't worry. Tomorrow I'm all yours."

He raised his eyebrows. "I like the sound of that."

I grinned. "It's your last night of freedom. What are you going to do?"

"Spend it thinking of you."

"I find that hard to believe."

"Well, we did agree, no strippers, remember?"

"I remember. I already told Stephanie." I shook my head. "I'm sure we'll just have some really good food."

"Sounds like a great way to spend the evening."

We leaned in to kiss. Before our lips had a chance to meet, a horn blared outside my apartment. Then a second horn sounded.

"Our rides are here." I laughed.

We walked out of the apartment together. Stephanie stuck her head out of the sunroof of a limousine.

"Wow! I wasn't expecting this!"

"Only the best for my bestie!" Stephanie winked at me and hopped out of the limo. She hugged me and then scowled at Max. "Aren't you supposed to be over there?" She pointed to the jeep filled with his friends.

"I'm going, I'm going!" He smiled at me.

"Okay, it's time to party!" Stephanie tugged me into the limousine.

I blew a kiss to Max as he was pulled into his friend's jeep. My heart tugged a little at the thought of him being out partying all night with his friends. It wasn't that I didn't trust him, it was just that most of the time, I'd rather spend my time with him.

Stephanie filled a glass of champagne for me and the

limo took off down the road. Soon I was swept up in the festivities. We had a delicious meal at one of the trendiest restaurants in town. As I ate the food I'd denied myself for so long, I made a few noises of appreciation.

"Wow, sounds like someone is practicing for the honeymoon." Stephanie winked. Everyone at the table laughed.

"I'm sorry, it's just so good! Food is good!"

Everyone laughed even louder. Stephanie leaned close. "Wait until you see what's for dessert."

"What do you mean?" I narrowed my eyes. All of a sudden the lights in the private room of the restaurant went out. "Is there a power outage?"

All of the women around me giggled. Then I heard a steady bass. It pounded through the room. One light clicked on. A man in a firefighter uniform stood in the light. He threw off his long jacket to reveal a perfect chest.

"No!"

"Isn't he beautiful?" Stephanie giggled.

"No!" I stood up from the table.

"Samantha, what's wrong?" The music got louder and the stripper began to dance.

"I promised Max no strippers, Stephanie, I told you that!"

"Oh, I didn't think you were serious." She frowned. "I'm sorry, I'll get rid of him."

I looked around at the disappointed expressions on

the faces of my friends. "No, it's fine. I'll just go for a walk. I need one after that meal anyway."

"Are you sure?"

"I'm sure." I smiled at her. "You ladies have fun." I stepped out of the restaurant on to a quiet street.

Despite the fact that I was in the city, the sky was clear enough to see a few stars. As I looked up at them, I basked in the knowledge that all of my wishes had been granted.

Not everything was perfect.

I still had no idea if Max was ever going to quit his job to work with me in my publishing business. I wasn't at my goal weight. I was also very far behind on a few chapters of my book. But I was excited about the future, and that to me, made it perfect.

Finally, I could see that life wasn't all about making everything perfect—it was about enjoying the bumps and the curves just as much as the straightaways. Max and I had so much in store for us. I couldn't wait to experience all that life had to offer with him by my side.

When I returned to the restaurant, the stripper was gone and my friends were quite red in the face.

"Fun?" I grinned.

"Fun." They all agreed.

We spent the rest of the evening enjoying drinks and swapping stories. It wasn't glamorous, but it was perfect for me.

By the time the limousine dropped me off late into

the night, I was overwhelmed with gratitude.

"Night, Stephanie. Thank you so much for everything." I hugged her.

"You're not mad about the stripper?"

"Not at all." I smiled. "The whole night was lovely."

"Enjoy your last night's sleep as a single woman, Samantha!"

I grinned. I liked the idea of that.

CHAPTER 29

I woke up the next morning and nearly jumped right out of my bed, I was so excited. I could barely stand the idea of waiting through the morning for our noon wedding.

It wasn't long before my apartment was filled with the women in my life—my mother, Stephanie, and a few bridesmaids. We shared a tasty brunch before we headed out to the garden.

To accommodate the reception, and to prepare for the wedding, we'd rented a small hall near Cerulean Gardens. I walked in and expected it to be just a regular room. Instead, it was filled with flowers and beautiful inspirational photographs.

"Wow!" I looked around at the surroundings with a wide smile.

"Do you like it?" Will stuck his head in the room.

"I do." I smiled at him. "Thank you, Will."

"My job is now done." He bowed to me. "A beautiful marriage you will have, I know you will."

"I know I will." My smile widened. He wiggled his

fingers in a quick wave, then disappeared.

A few minutes later Stephanie and my mother stepped into the room.

"Ready to get ready?" My mother held up a curling iron, a pack of bobby pins, and a camera.

"Let's do this." I nodded.

After I was primped and photographed, it was time to put on the dress. Stephanie carried the dress bag in and prepared it for me to put on. As I slid into it my mother helped to slide the sleeves over my arms.

"You look amazing." My mother's eyes brimmed with tears. She cupped my cheeks and kissed the tip of my nose. "I can't believe it's finally happening."

"Me either." My heart fluttered so fast that I thought I might pass out. I tried to practice some of the deep breathing exercises I'd learned in meditation class.

"You're going to be great." Stephanie wiped away her own tears. "What a wonderful moment. Thank you for letting me share it with you."

"There's no one else in the world that I would want to be at my side." I hugged her.

"Okay, ladies." Will stuck his head into the room. "The music is playing."

I took a deep breath and nodded.

I saw my flower girl run by with a basket full of flower petals. A high giggle escaped her. The sound reflected what I felt inside—excited, giddy, and as if all my wishes had finally come true.

As my bridesmaids lined up to walk down the aisle, there was no question in my mind that marrying Max was what I wanted above anything else that I'd ever dreamed of.

Stephanie gave me a quick smile before she began walking down the aisle as well. The beautiful gardens that surrounded me made the moment even more magical.

I took a deep breath and took my first step down the aisle. I waited for the sky to fall in, or for me to trip and fall, or for my dress to tear, but none of that happened. Instead, I met the eyes of the man of my dreams.

Max smiled at me in a way that I'd never seen before. His lips were parted and his eyes wide, and his smile spread as if it might never end. In his expression, I finally saw just how beautiful he thought I was. The sight warmed my heart and brought tears to my eyes. All of the time I'd wasted on feeling insecure—he honestly considered me the most beautiful woman on earth. I knew that now. I saw that in his eyes more than ever before.

As I took the next step down the aisle, I was lost in his eyes. I didn't hear the music. I didn't see the smiling faces. He held my gaze the entire way.

When I reached him, he held his hand out to me. I accepted it. On instinct I leaned in and kissed him full on the lips. The crowd erupted with laughter and applause.

The minister leaned forward and spoke in a soft voice. "Uh, we have a few matters we're supposed to attend to before the kiss."

"I'm so sorry!" My cheeks burned with embarrassment.

"I'm not." Max grinned. He wrapped his arm around my waist and leaned me back as he offered me a sweet but passionate kiss.

"That's it—I guess I'm not needed here." The minister tossed his hands in the air and laughed.

When everyone settled, the ceremony continued. It was simple and sweet and I didn't hear a word of it. I was too busy staring at Max.

"Now, Max, you may finally kiss your bride!"

Our lips met in a quick soft kiss.

As we walked down the aisle together, our friends showered us with something that I thought was rice. Then I noticed that it wasn't rice at all. It was birdseed!

"I bet this is Will's doing!" Max laughed.

"Hurry, before they get you." I grabbed his hand and we ran for the car.

CHAPTER 30

The reception was one big party. The music was loud, the drinks were flowing, and the dance floor was packed. Max and I danced, and danced, and danced some more. Our pre-marriage kisses were the talk of the crowd. The food was wonderful.

When it came time for the cake, I realized I had no idea what flavor it would be.

"Do you know what we're eating?" I asked Max as we sliced the cake.

"I think Will picked it."

"White chocolate raspberry truffle." We both spoke at the same time and then laughed.

"Don't worry, I'll be on my best behavior." Max smiled and fed me a dainty bite of cake.

"Very good." I smiled as I savored the cake. "Now it's my turn." I took the plate, snatched up the piece of cake, and smashed it right in his face.

"Sammy!"

"Revenge is mine!" I laughed and picked up my dress

as I ran.

He chased me across the dance floor with the crumbs that remained on the plate.

When it was time to leave, I was even more excited. I would finally find out where our honeymoon would be. All I knew was that we were flying, but not where we were flying to.

I ducked into the private room to change.

I stood in front of the tall mirror. Maybe it was the way it was tilted, or maybe it was the glow of knowing that I was now married to Max, but I thought I looked beautiful.

I smoothed my hand over the intricate lace of the gown. I couldn't believe that I'd ever considered buying a different dress. It was perfect and a treasure that I'd keep with me always.

As I gazed at myself in the mirror, all of my insecurities melted away.

This was me, no matter what size, no matter what dress—this was the Sammy who was finally truly happy with herself. I smiled at my reflection.

"Can I come in?"

My heart raced at the sound of Max's voice outside the door. My husband's voice. It made me giddy with excitement to be able to think of him that way.

"Sure, come in."

I watched in the mirror as he stepped inside the small room. Dressed in his tuxedo, he was handsome in a way that consumed all of my senses. He paused just inside the door and stared at me.

"I'm never going to forget the way you look tonight."

"That's funny, I was just thinking the same thing." I laughed. "Do you want to help me unzip? I need to get changed for the drive to the airport. It might help if I knew what I should change into."

"Oh? Then good thing I brought this." He held up a small gift bag and smiled at me.

"What's that?" I turned to face him.

"It's a surprise." He wiggled it around in front of me with a wild grin.

I snatched at the bag and laughed when he whipped it out of my grasp.

"Aren't you going to give it to me?"

"Yes." He reached up and ran a hand along my shoulders until he found the zipper of my dress. He eased it down enough so that I'd be able to step out of it. "But only if you promise me something."

I started to turn to look at him, but he steered me in the direction of the mirror. "Will you do that?"

"What do you want me to promise?" I asked, looking at his reflection in the mirror.

"That you'll wear it—no arguments." He held my gaze in the mirror.

"Can't I take a peek first?" I grinned.

"Do you trust me, Sammy?" He kissed the side of my neck.

"You know I do."

"Do you know that I love you?" He kissed the other side of my neck.

"Yes, I do."

"Then promise me, you'll wear it." His eyes shimmered in the mirror. Was it the light in the room reflected off the glass or the excitement he felt? I wasn't sure.

"Okay." I swallowed hard. "I promise."

"Wonderful." He held out the bag to me. "You probably won't need it until we get there. You don't have to worry about packing, Stephanie already did that for you."

"Oh, that's why she was snooping in my closet!" I laughed.

Max wiggled his eyebrows and kissed my cheek. "I can't wait to spend the rest of my life with you, Sammy." He smiled and walked out of the room.

I couldn't wait a second longer to look into the bag. When I saw what was inside, my jaw dropped. Of all the things I'd expected it might be, this was not it.

I pulled out a stylish navy blue bikini bathing suit. I couldn't remember a time in my life that I'd ever worn a bikini.

"No way! I can't wear this!"

I thought about calling Max back to explain to him why I couldn't and then it hit me.

Max was proud of me. My husband was proud of my

body and he wanted me to show it off. Was that such a terrible thing?

I smiled at the thought of feeling the water and the sun striking parts of my body that were usually covered up. Still, the thought of being so exposed—with what I still considered a less than perfect body—made my heart race.

But I'd made a promise—the first promise of our marriage. I hoped I would be brave enough to keep it.

"Well, I guess we're going somewhere warm." I smiled and grabbed the change of clothes that I'd packed. I slipped out of my dress and left it on the hanger beside the mirror. Stephanie had promised to take care of everything for me.

After I changed, I headed out the door to meet Max, the gift bag dangling from my finger, ready to begin the first of many adventures with my husband—with my best friend and the love of my life.

A NOTE FROM THE AUTHOR

Fictional character, Samantha Bradford and the Single Wide Female books are written for every woman out there who has struggled with their weight, self-esteem and any number of issues that we all face as we work to become the best versions of ourselves that we can be.

These books are meant to be light-hearted and fun, with the hope that they will also inspire you to make your own "bucket list" of sorts—and to REALLY live your life to the fullest, loving yourself completely as you do so.

Lillianna loves to hear from her readers and can be contacted via her website where you can also download a complimentary book.

LilliannaBlake.com

ALL TITLES BY LILLIANNA BLAKE

http://Amazon.com/author/lilliannablake
*Check the author page for current list of titles

Single Wide Female in Love

Single Wide Female: The Bucket List

#17 Host a Dinner Party
#18 Publish a Book
#19 Walk Across Hot Coals
#20 Learn to Swim
#21 Learn to Meditate
#22 Quit My Job
#23 Learn to Salsa
#24 Fall in Love

Other Single Wide Female Titles
My Valentine's Day
St. Paddy's Day Disaster
A Bunny Tale
Sammy's Christmas List

Becoming Zara
*how the B.I.G. Girls Club came to be

B.I.G. Girls Club
The Rockstar's Girlfriend
The Former Model

Visit the author website at LilliannaBlake.com to get on the notification list for new releases and to receive a complimentary book to learn what inspired Sammy to begin her bucket list.

www.ingramcontent.com/pod-product-compliance
Lightning Source LLC
Chambersburg PA
CBHW070549180626
46817CB00005B/1758